The Heartbreaker

Nicole Higginbotham-Hogue

.

Published by Nicole Higginbotham-Hogue, 2024.

THE HEARTBREAKER

First edition. February 6, 2024.

ISBN: 979-8223383239

Written by Nicole Higginbotham-Hogue.

Table of Contents

Chapter One

"Penny, I can't do this anymore," Henry said, looking into my eyes. "I mean, I love you, but I don't think we are compatible."

I looked back at him. I think he was expecting me to dispute this claim, but I felt the same way. Henry and I had grown to be comfortable, not compatible. I didn't understand it. We had done all the things normal couples do. We had dated. We had created our own friends group. We had even been intimate, but the connection wasn't there.

Every relationship that I had experienced went this way. First, there was a period of excitement when you first got together. There were surprise dates, flowers, and a period where you just asked each other questions about anything and everything that came to mind.

Then, things got more serious. You had your first fight and found out your differences and decided if you were willing to put in the effort to understand each other. This period of time seemed to be the make it or break it period for most couples, but I was persistent, so I usually made it past this uncomfortable stage.

After the first fights and the period where the two people learn to communicate, there is a period where the two of you decide what your goals are and where you want to be as a couple. You start to build a future together, and you watch your dreams come to fruition.

Then, there is a period of comfort, where your life has intersected with the other person's, and usually, this is where most couples reflect on their accomplishments and enjoy their mutual success. However, it was usually during this period of time that I realized I was bored and wanted out.

No man had been able to hold my interest. I got bored easily, and I stayed to see if things would change. But it was the same story every time. I was bored out of my mind with the relationship. I always expected to experience something new, something more exciting, like in the movies. Then, reality hit. Love like that didn't exist.

Love was based on commitment and work, not connection, and I just got bored with the monotony of it. I don't even know why I kept trying. It seemed like such a waste of time. I guess somewhere inside of me I wanted to feel a connection with another person that was real, one that I would feel bad about losing, but whatever that connection was, I hadn't found it yet.

"Penny?" Henry inquired. "Are you going to say anything?"

I had already forgotten that we were having the conversation and gotten lost in my own thoughts. "Yes," I replied, doing my best to be polite. "I hope that you have a nice life, Henry, and I hope that you find someone that treats you right."

Henry kept looking at me, like he expected something more, but I didn't have more to give. "You can keep the house if you want," I said, trying to make him feel better. "I'll call and have my name removed."

"Don't you want it?" He asked, almost in tears at this point. "We spent the last two years of our lives there. It has a lot of memories."

Memories. Just the thing I wanted to leave behind. "No, you can have it," I said, knowing that I wouldn't want to relive the memories that we had together.

"Okay," Henry said, looking down at the ground. "Have the real estate company send over the paperwork and I'll sign it so you can get your name off."

"No problem," I said, hoping the conversation was over. "I really do hope you have a good life."

Chapter Two

"**Y**ou're so heartless," my best friend Rosita said as she helped me carry boxes of my belongings into her house.

I had told her everything that went down with Henry, and how he seemed upset when I didn't want the house. Somehow, she had determined that I was the one at fault. This didn't surprise me. Rosita had always liked Henry, and she had often told me that I was mean to him.

It wasn't like I went out of my way to be mean though. I just spoke my truth, and Henry didn't seem to like it. We had never really gotten on equal footing with each other. We both had just shoved things under the rug until it bulged like an anthill. That was no way to live or coexist.

Henry deserved better. He was a good guy with a good job and an education to match. Most women would be happy with just that, but those things didn't really fill my heart. I needed something more. I wasn't sure where I would find it or what exactly it was, but I knew it wasn't Henry.

"So, we are going to put a majority of this in the garage, right?" Rosita asked, pointing to the stack of boxes she had carried in.

"Yes," I replied. "I am only staying here until I find out if I was accepted into the internship program in California or get a new place, but until I get a yes or no on the internship, I don't want to invest my time and money into looking for an apartment."

"That seems reasonable," Rosita replied. "It would suck to find an apartment you love only to find out that you won't be in town to enjoy it."

"My thoughts exactly," I replied. "Besides, I don't want to pay for an apartment if I am going to be out of town. I already have to pay for college. I don't know if my budget could handle paying for my out of town expenses and rent for an apartment I had here."

"Yea, that's not the best move after leaving a relationship," Rosita said. "You might as well get comfortable here while you are waiting for the internship program to reply. At least then you can invest your money in a safer way."

"Right," I said, picking up a few boxes. "Do you want these in the corner of your garage so you can still park your car?"

"That would be great," Rosita said. "It will be easier to find them if we have to move them that way too."

"Yeah, I don't want to have to go on a scavenger hunt to find the boxes," I agreed. I started walking towards the side door that led to the garage. It was nice that Rosita was going to let me store my stuff at her house. It had saved me a pretty penny in storage costs.

I turned on the garage light and found an empty space in the back of the garage by a tool bench and piled the boxes neatly in the space. I wanted to be the best guest that I could be while I stayed at her house. I didn't want to cause any issues or get in her way.

I went back in the house to get more boxes. The quicker I could get everything put away, the quicker I could relax. I had a lot of things to think of after leaving Henry. It had been a while since I was on my own, and I was finally getting a chance to plan my new future the way I saw fit.

Chapter Three

"If you need anything, you know where to find me," Rosita called as she walked to her bedroom.

"Okay, Rosita," I called back. "Thank you again for letting me stay here."

"Anytime love," Rosita said, going into her room and closing the door.

I waited for the house to grow silent and then stretched out on the couch. I really had no direct long-term plan, and that kind of scared me. I was used to being organized and prepared. I usually had a routine that I followed, and there weren't too many surprises that tripped it up.

However, now I felt like I was all over the place. I wasn't in my own home, in my own bed. I had boxes in someone else's garage, and I was sleeping on a couch, waiting to find out where I would be during the summer. I wasn't a fan of not having a routine, and I couldn't stand not knowing what was going to happen next. It made me anxious and uncertain if I was moving in the right direction.

I turned on the television and muted it so it didn't wake up Rosita. I needed something to distract me from my current situation. The uncertainty of knowing if I was ever going to end up in a situation where I was happy was getting to me, and I didn't want to start having second thoughts about how I handled the situation with Henry. I couldn't afford to take another step backwards. I had already set myself back on achieving my dreams and my goals.

I watched the show on the television, doing my best to get into the plot. It was some sitcom with four friends in New York who kept doing silly things. I let the humor ease my mind, and I felt sleep slowly approaching. I let my eyes slowly hide behind my eyelids, all thoughts and worries, dissipating.

· · · ·

MY ALARM WENT OFF AND I jumped out of bed, but since I wasn't in the bed I was used to, I ended up landing smack dab on a hardwood floor. I got up, rubbing the arm I had landed on and took a moment to remember where I was. The memory of going to Rosita's house slowly drifted through my mind and with it the memory of breaking up with Henry. I remembered the sad look on Henry's face and how he almost looked disappointed when I didn't fight for the relationship.

I felt bad. That's not how I had wanted to start the morning. I wanted to be focused. I wanted to move forward, but instead, I felt my emotions taking over. Stop it, I told myself. I didn't have time to pity myself or look back on the past, even if everything had happened less than twenty-four hours ago. I had things to do. I had classes to attend and an internship to check up on.

I took myself to the bathroom. Maybe, a hot shower would calm my mind. I didn't want my entire life to fall to shambles because I couldn't control my emotions. I needed to be strong. I still had an opportunity to get my foot in the door in the business world. I just needed to be able to pick myself off the ground and dust myself off.

I started the shower and urged my brain to remember all the things I needed to do to prepare myself for class. I had packed a couple of suits that still needed pressed, and I had even bought a new pair of heels for the last week of class. Maybe, if I looked the part, I would feel the part. I wasn't sure if that was the case, but I sure was willing to try.

Chapter Four

I drove to the university and did my best to find a parking spot. It was usually busy at this time, so finding a place to park was difficult unless you wanted to park in a store parking lot and walk to class. A car finally squeezed out of one of the small parking spots in front of the university, and I took no time in taking the space. I could hear the other cars around me honk their horns, upset that they hadn't seen the spot first.

I ignored the noise, picked up my binder, and locked my car. I didn't have time to deal with the chaotic emotions of morning traffic. I had a class to get to, and I didn't want to be late. I always did my best to get ready and on the road forty-five minutes before my class started. I knew that it left a good impression to be on time, and it also gave me time to prepare myself before the lecture started.

I walked across the campus, waving at people that I knew and headed toward the large brick building, where the business classes took place. As I entered the building, I saw a woman named Debby from my class coming up to me. I didn't know her personally, but we always sat together in class, so we could point out the other students that didn't take the time to dress right or grasp the material. We didn't intend to be mean by doing this. We were being realistic. No one goes to a business class in jeans and a T-shirt and expects to be successful in business. Everything is about presentation and appearance.

"How are you doing?" Debby asked, looking me up and down. "You must have had a hard night. I have never seen you so disheveled."

I looked down at my outfit. I had a pinstriped suit on with a dark camisole underneath the jacket. I had worn pantyhose, which was barely visible beneath my pants, and I had put on a fresh pair of black heels. I had given myself a once over in the mirror, and I hadn't seen anything out of place, so clearly I was off my game if Debby had noticed.

"I'm not talking about your attire," Debby said, locking her gaze on my eyes. "I'm talking about your nonverbal expression. You look like you just went through the ringer."

"Is it that noticeable?" I asked, a little embarrassed. I didn't believe in mixing business and pleasure, so I had done my best to keep the turmoil of the night before away from my educational life.

"It's only noticeable if you look closely," Debby said. "But I can see you are upset about something. You usually hold your head high and you just have a flare about yourself. Today, you look like someone sunk your ship."

"Hm," I said. "I'm not sure. I was worried about getting a parking spot so I could get to class on time, but besides that, I haven't really had any issues this morning."

"Hm," Debby said, looking somewhat disappointed that I didn't open up further.

What she didn't know was that I wasn't going to open up about my emotional life at school. If I wanted people to know that I was a strong leader, it was important that I didn't get close to too many people. I couldn't go about letting everyone know what my struggles were. That would give them a reason to squish me while I was down. I just had to put on a smile and go about my day like nothing happened.

Chapter Five

lass was uneventful give or take a few dirty looks that I had gotten from my colleagues for answering questions that they didn't know the answers to. Time went by fast, and eventually the class was let out. As I walked towards the door, I heard the professor calling my name. I walked towards the older man that was wearing his signature black suit and gray tie and gave him my best smile.

"Yes, Professor Edwards," I said, sweetly. I had never gotten in trouble for anything at school, and I hadn't missed any classes, so I figured the only thing he could be calling me down for was the internship that I had applied for.

I had waited so long to find out if I had gotten into the internship that just waiting for him to continue the conversation made me hold my breath. What if I didn't get in? What if my grades aren't high enough? Just because I was top of my class here, didn't mean that I was top of the class in comparison to other students going to other universities.

There were only four spots available in the internship program, and those that got in were to be flown to San Francisco in order to work with students from the university there that owned their own businesses. I knew that if I could work with a student from the University of San Francisco who already had a business going that I could get a permanent position at their company. It might take a lot of hard work and I might have to sacrifice a summer doing it, but in the end it would be worth my time.

"Miss Brookington, I had a letter sent to me regarding an internship that you applied for," Professor Edwards said. "I'm not sure why it was mailed to me, but I figured that it would be best to let you open it."

"Thank you, Professor," I said, doing my best to keep my countenance. I didn't want to be one of those women that got overly excited.

"Well, here you are, Miss," the professor said, handing me the letter. "I suppose I won't find out the contents of this mysterious letter as we are on the verge of summer break, but I do hope it brings promising news."

"I appreciate it," I said, smiling at the professor. "Have a nice summer, sir."

"You as well," the professor said, and I headed towards the exit to find a quiet place where I could open the letter and determine what my future held. I was either going to get an opportunity of a lifetime to work under someone that already knew the business world and what it entailed or I was going to have to find a summer job and a new apartment here and hope that there would be another opportunity to get my foot in the door.

I found a quiet corner in the spacious building where the foot traffic was minimal and slowly opened the sealed letter. Once the letter was out of the envelope, I left it folded for a moment, scared to open it. I had worked so hard to get into this internship. It would be a big blow if I was rejected. I took a deep breath and slowly unfolded the piece of paper, skimming through the text on the front.

I had been accepted. Relief washed over me as I read these words. I was going to get the chance to start over. I might have failed in the relationship world, but in the business world, I had just taken a giant step forward. Now, I had the chance to do something with my life. I wasn't a failure after all.

Chapter Six

C lasses had ended and I was motivated to go back to Rosita's and get myself ready to leave town. I needed to get a storage unit unless Rosita was able to house my boxes while I was out of town. I wanted to call my parents and let them know the good news, and I needed to figure out what I was going to do with my online customers during the summer.

I already owned my own business. It was an online clothing resale store, but it didn't make enough money to pay the bills. I did my best with the time that I had to give attention to my small business. However, with school and the duties that I had when I was with Henry, I could never give it my full attention.

In order to run the business, I had to go to thrift stores and repurpose used clothes. Then, I took a picture of the item, put it online, and my community of followers would pick the items they wanted to buy and purchase them from my online store front. I had to run advertisements on social media and pay for big ad companies to share my website as well, but since I already had a low budget to work with and a limited amount of time, I didn't usually get enough advertisements out to attract a wide array of customers.

I was hoping that the internship would help me find a better direction for my efforts. I wanted to run a successful business. I didn't want to just scrape by. Both of my parents were highly successful individuals. They were both at the top of their companies, and they had managed to give me a beautiful life. In fact, I had really never had to pay for anything of my own until I was an adult.

Now, I still had their financial support, but I was working towards being able to be more independent. I wanted to show my parents that I could be successful too. I wanted them to know that I could take care of myself, and I wanted to prove to them that I didn't need a man to do it for me. My mom was insistent that I find a man with a good job to help support my lifestyle. It wasn't that she didn't have confidence in me. She just didn't think that I was going to be able to make enough money on my own to live the life that I wanted.

My mom loved Henry. In fact, she had already begun to make wedding plans for the two of us. She loved the fact that Henry had a good job and a nice house, and she had thought that he would be the father of her future grandchildren. Once I had gotten with him, my mom seemed at peace. It was like she knew that I would be taken care of despite my success or failure in the business world.

Now that I was single again, I knew that my mom would be on my back about getting a new boyfriend or getting back with Henry. She seemed to think that I needed to concentrate on my relationships in order to achieve financial success. This made me feel bad, because if I failed at anything, it was relationships, and I wished that she understood that I might be better on my own than with someone that I wasn't happy being with.

"You just have to try," my mother would say. "You have to make it work."

I would argue that my happiness is more important, and she would argue back that happiness isn't all about being content with the man you are with. She would say it is about getting along and watching your goals work so you can get the future you want. Arguments like these made me wonder if my mom was happy. Did she just marry my dad for financial security or were they in love? Did my mom even know what love was?

Chapter Seven

Rosita wasn't home from work when I got to her house, so I used the time alone to get into a more comfortable outfit and call local storage units so I could price them out. When she still didn't come home after that, I decided that it might be a good time to let my parents know about the internship and that I would be out of town for a while. I knew that they would be happy about the internship, but I also knew that my mom would ask about Henry. That was a bridge that I wasn't sure I wanted to cross at the moment.

I took a deep breath and dialed their home phone, hoping that my dad picked up the phone before my mom did. It was a long shot as I knew that my dad didn't like to talk on the phone, but I figured the conversation would go smoothly if I was talking to him. The phone rang a couple of times and just when I thought that it was going to go to voicemail, I heard it pick up.

"Hello, darling," my mom's voice rang through the receiver. "What are you up to?"

"Nothing much," I replied. "I just got home from school, and I decided that it might be a good time to call you."

"I see," my mom replied. "How's Henry doing?"

I grimaced. "Henry seems to be doing fine," I replied.

"Seems to be doing?" my mom asked. "What does that mean? Aren't you with Henry right now?"

"No," I said. "We broke up."

Silence broke out on the other end of the phone, and I knew that my mother was mulling it over. Finally, she came back.

"Why did you break up, dear?" my mom asked. "I thought that the two of you were happy. I was even in the midst of planning your wedding. I told all of the women at the country club about it."

"Well, it sounds like you got a little ahead of yourself," I said. "Henry and I weren't in a perfect place. We were arguing all the time. It just wasn't working."

"Sometimes you need to give a little to get a little," my mom said. "Henry had a lot going for himself. He was educated. He had a good job. He was very polite."

"And he was boring," I replied. "I can't commit to spending the rest of my life with a boring man. I need some kind of zest in my relationship."

"Zest is for the movies," my mom said. "Real relationships are much different. There are fights and struggles, but then there are goals that the two of you build so you can get the things that you want."

"What if the thing that I want is happiness?" I asked. "What if it isn't a material thing?"

"Well, that's something that you find in yourself," my mom replied.

"I see," I said. I was tired of arguing. "Well, I just wanted to call you to let you know that I will be leaving town for a few months. I got accepted into an internship at the University of San Francisco."

"Congratulations, honey!" my mom said. "Maybe, you will meet a nice guy in California. You never know. I hear men down there are more open with their emotions. Maybe, you will find the zest that you have been looking for."

I put my head in my hand while I listened to my mom go on and on about the men in California. She had said nothing about the fact that I might get a new job. She said nothing about how educational it would be. She was just concerned about me finding a new man.

Chapter Eight

B y the time that Rosita got home, I had already called my mom, priced storage units, and put an announcement on my website that I would be out of town for the summer. I felt somewhat accomplished, but I also knew that I still had to pack. I was sitting on the couch, trying to take a moment to myself when Rosita came into the room.

"So, how was your day?" she asked, handing me a plate of take-out food.

"It was good," I said with a smile. "I just found out that I got accepted into the internship that I applied for, so now, I just have to figure out storage and packing."

"Well, you can keep your stuff in the garage if you want," Rosita said. "Then, when you get back and get a new place, we can just move it there."

"I appreciate that," I said. "I'm trying to show my parents that I can handle this break-up and take care of myself, and if I don't have to ask them for money, it will help prove my point."

"It's always good to be self-sufficient," Rosita commented. "And you'll get it. It just takes some time. So, what do your parents think about you taking the internship?"

"Well, my mom was more focused on the fact that Henry and I broke up, and I didn't get the chance to talk to my dad," I said. "It seems like if I had married Henry, my mom would have been happier."

"She didn't say anything about the internship?" Rosita asked, somewhat concerned.

"She told me that I need to look into California guys while I am down there," I replied, rolling my eyes. "She still seems to think that the only way I am going to survive is by getting a man."

"That's so sad," Rosita said. "You would think that she would be proud that her daughter has managed to launch her own business and

15

is now getting the chance to go further in the business world by participating in an exclusive internship. I'm proud of you. I don't know if I could do it."

"I appreciate that, Rosita," I said. "But mom is old-school, and even though she has had success in her own career, she still thinks that the security of having a man is the only way a woman is going to get through this world. I really wish she would be more open-minded. I wish she could see that I am just as good on my own as I am when I am in a relationship."

"Me too," Rosita said. "Because pushing you to find a man might put you in a situation where you end up with the wrong one. A relationship isn't a security deposit. It's a chance for two individuals that love and care for each other to work together on their goals."

"She said something about goals too," I said. "But if I'm going to find love, it's going to be found in the heart first."

Rosita nodded and we finished our dinner and got ready to go to bed. "You'll find what you are looking for in due time," Rosita said before going into her bedroom. "I think that you are taking the right approach with this. Patience is a virtue."

"Thanks," I said to my friend before laying down on the couch. It wasn't very often that someone said I was doing the right thing with my love life, and I held Rosita's words close to my heart. I closed my eyes, thinking about the trip ahead of me. I had never been to California. Maybe, I would find a different life there.

Chapter Nine

I woke up early, knowing that I had to pack for my trip. I had one day left until it was go time, and I still hadn't looked through the boxes in the garage to see if there was anything in there that I needed. I went to the bathroom, grabbed some clothes that I had stored in a laundry basket near the couch and began to get dressed.

Rosita was at work again today. She had switched shifts so she could take me to the airport the following day. I really was thankful to have her around. She was making this transition easy and stress free, but Rosita was just that kind of person. She cared about those around her, and she was the type of friend that would do almost anything for you. I was blessed to have her in my life. I didn't have that many close friends, so having one that cared as much as she did made me feel loved.

I did my hair and brushed my teeth, knowing that I had to get ready fast so I would have time to go through everything and pack. I had almost checked off everything that I needed to do before leaving town off my list. I just needed to reorganize the belongings that I had brought in from Henry and my old house and separate the things that I needed for this new trip.

Just as I opened the door to the garage, I felt my phone start to vibrate in my pocket. I pulled it out, looked at the receiver, and saw Henry's name flash across the screen. If anything, this was the worst time for Henry to call me. I had so much to do, and every minute counted. However, I figured if he was calling me then it must be an urgent matter as the two of us hadn't really spoken since we had parted ways.

"Hello," I said, answering the phone.

"Hi, Bunny," Henry said, using the pet name he had created for me during the time we were together.

I was a little thrown off by this as we were no longer a unit, and I decided not to reply.

"Are you still there?" Henry asked, an overwhelmed tone in his voice.

"Yes," I said, hoping that he would get to the point so I could get on with my life.

"I've missed you," Henry said. "The house doesn't feel the same without you there."

"I'm sorry about that," I said. I didn't know what to say. I didn't miss him. I didn't miss the house, and I didn't miss the life that we had made together. I was happy to be on my own.

"Aren't you going to say that you miss me too?" Henry inquired.

"No," I replied. "I'm not going to lie to you. I'm happier on my own. I feel more like myself than I have in years."

I didn't mean to be so harsh, but I knew that it would do no good to lie to him. I was happier. I didn't want to get back together, and I didn't want to lead him on. I was confident that the two of us had made the right choice in breaking up. I certainly didn't want to take a step backward.

"Oh, okay," Henry said. "Well, that's what I called for. I just wanted to see how you were doing and let you know that I missed you being around."

"Okay," I replied. "Thank you for letting me know. Have a good life, Henry." I hung up the receiver and took a deep breath. I wasn't going to get pulled back into that mess again.

Chapter Ten

The next day, Rosita and I headed to the airport early in the morning. I was a little nervous as I knew this experience might be one that changed my life and I was doing my best to stay calm. Rosita parked in the airport parking lot, and I gave her money so she could pay the toll when she went to leave. She had already done so much for me. I didn't want to leave her paying fees that technically belonged to me.

We walked in the airport and I got checked in. Then, Rosita followed me to the airport security area. I gave her a big hug and thanked her before getting in line, and she told me that if I needed her to send anything to me in California, she would. I felt a little tear side down my cheek as she left. Of course, I wiped it away quickly so it didn't smear my make-up, but that was the first time that I had cried upon leaving town.

I think it was just such a sentimental moment. Rosita had been the only one there when I needed someone. Even my own mom was more concerned about my finances and love life than my emotional state. Rosita had understood me. She knew exactly what to do too. I'm not exactly sure how I was blessed enough to become friends with her, but I was glad that I was. Sometimes, it was as if she was the only person that truly cared about me.

Though I knew I wasn't the nicest person, I was even worse before I met Rosita. The two of us had crossed paths one day when I was looking at fabric at a craft store. We both had tried to grab the same piece of fabric, and that had resulted in a long conversation about fashion and the evolution of style. I had never met someone that loved fashion as much as I did before then. That was long before I had met Debbie from my class, and I had decided to take Rosita out for coffee so we could continue our conversation.

After that day, Rosita and I spent more time together. She was single, and I had never seen her date anyone. So, I figured that her love life wasn't her top priority. That made me more comfortable with her, because I knew that she wouldn't be pushing me to go out on double dates and so forth. Instead of focusing on the stuff that other people our age were focused on like dating and going out to clubs, we decided to spend our time at fashion shows and crafting jewelry and accessories.

When I got with Henry, Rosita grew close to him as well. I was happy that the two of them got along, but I was a little jealous of their bond. I hadn't really wanted to share Rosita with him. It just seemed too personal, and though I was dating him, I just didn't feel like opening my whole life to him. So, when I broke up with Henry, I knew Rosita would be devastated. She had grown used to having him around. I had wondered how this dynamic would change our friendship, and I was glad when I found out that despite the break-up, she still wanted me around.

Though I had many acquaintances, Rosita was one of the few that I considered a true friend. I was able to talk to her about almost anything without being judged, and she truly understood me as a person. It was nice to have someone that saw you as you and not the stereotype that everyone else had created.

Chapter Eleven

I made it through security and onto the plane. By that time, I was so overwhelmed with emotion that it wasn't funny. I was thinking about the life that I was leaving behind. I really disliked that life. It was full of expectations set by other people and unfulfilling romantic relationships. I was ready for something new.

I thought about Henry and how he had called me before I left. I didn't understand it. Though Henry and I had been together for a couple of years, we never really bonded. He didn't know my deep, dark secrets. He didn't know what made me cry. He knew the basics. He knew my favorite drink and where I liked to go to dinner. He knew where I liked to shop and he knew that I ran a business but he didn't really know too much about it.

Henry was a primary example of how my love life had gone. I had wasted a lot of time on men that didn't care about what I was thinking about or how I felt. They didn't know the real me. They just knew what was on top, and though you would think they would dig deeper with time, none of them took the effort to do so.

I felt plastic, like a Barbie. It was as if I existed just so they had something to play with. They gave me money and they got what they wanted. I couldn't live like that. I wasn't willing to sacrifice all of my internal thoughts and dreams just to look good for a man that didn't give two shits about what I was thinking. I knew I could do better. I just didn't know what I was looking for.

I looked out the window, watching the clouds float by and wondered how I would get along in California. Rosita wasn't going to be there, so I wouldn't have the support from her that I had grown used to. I didn't always get along with others on a personal level, so that made me a little apprehensive. I knew that it would be important to make friends, especially if I was going to live so far from home, but I had grown out of practice. I had been so busy making sure that I had a good reputation that I hadn't really gotten close to those around me. What if I couldn't make friends? What if they just thought I was a stuck-up bitch?

I wasn't the type of person that kissed anyone's ass or buttered things up. I was direct and honest. A lot of people didn't like that trait. They thought that I was being judgemental and mean. So, if I was going to make friends in California, I was going to have to find someone that understood who I was and didn't get easily offended. Hopefully, there would be someone there that got me.

I took a deep breath, trying to relax. After thinking about my love life and my friendships and this big life change, I was overwhelmed. Maybe, I hadn't made the right choice after all. Though taking this internship would be great for my career, it might not be the best choice when it came to my wellbeing.

I closed my eyes, trying to calm myself further. I didn't want to panic now. I was already almost there. There was no turning back. I had already said my goodbyes. I had already packed. I just needed to get there. Even if I had made a bad choice, it was my responsibility to deal with it. I couldn't just turn my back on my obligations, even if my anxiety was high.

Chapter Twelve

The plane landed and I followed everyone down the stairs and into the terminal. The weather in California looked nice, which was a nice change of pace from what I had experienced back home. It was warm and inviting, and it looked like a place I could get used to. I walked to baggage claim, grabbing a trolley so I could get all my bags out the door. I had tried to pack as much stuff as I could. I didn't want to be caught off guard if I needed something specific, and I wanted to have enough outfits to last me, especially if I was going to be in a work environment.

After loading my bags, I pushed my trolley out the door so I could look for the shuttle that was supposed to pick me up. I had searched for a baggage attendant to help me with the unloading and loading process, but there were none in sight. So, I pushed the trolley in my pin-point heels and skirt, hoping not to fall before I got to the shuttle. The process wasn't easy, and I had to focus as I moved the trolley around the crowd of people walking around me.

Finally, I saw four women, holding a sign welcoming interns. All of the women looked put together and beautiful. "Hello," I said, greeting the women as I approached the shuttle.

"Hello," a blonde woman said, coming over to me. "Do you need help with these bags?"

"Please," I replied. "I didn't know what to bring, and I didn't want to inconvenience anybody by having to ask for anything."

"You're fine," the woman laughed. "I'm Brittney. What's your name?"

"Penny," I replied.

"Well, Penny I'm sure that you are pretty pooped after your flight," Brittney said. "Let's get these bags on, and we can get to the dorms so you can get more comfortable."

"I really do appreciate it," I said. "You have no idea what it took to get me here."

"No worries," Brittneyreplied. She turned to look over her shoulder, calling another woman that looked similar to her in appearance. "Christina! Will you give me a hand with these bags?"

The other woman came over, and Brittney and her quickly unloaded the bags off the cart and onto the shuttle.

"There you are," Brittney said. "Why don't you take a seat on the shuttle? We will be taking off soon."

I thanked Brittney again for her hospitality, and I walked onto the shuttle. There were already a few women that had boarded. One in particular caught my eye. She was dark-skinned with curly, black hair and brown eyes. I could tell by the smile on her face that she wasn't nervous about the internship, and she didn't seem to be intimidated by anyone around her. Though she was a woman, she had masculine features. Her tight T-shirt squeezed a pair of muscular arms, and her body language reminded me more of the men that I had been around than any woman I had ever seen. I was intrigued. I didn't understand why I was so taken with the woman, but I was.

I walked to the back of the shuttle, passing the interesting woman as I did. I wanted to be in a position to watch people without being noticed. I needed to know more about the woman in the black T-shirt. I wanted to know her name, her interests, and why that smile of hers gave me butterflies in my stomach. The woman that I was interested in suddenly turned around and began to introduce herself to others. This was my chance.

Chapter Thirteen

I watched as the woman in the black T-shirt made rounds introducing herself to others. I had learned that her name was Rica and she was from New York. I had wondered where that accent had come from. I had been to New York a time or two in the past, but Rica's accent was a mixture of the regular New York accent and something else. I couldn't quite put my finger on it.

I waited patiently for Rica to come up to me like she had everyone else, but she sat down as soon as the shuttle began moving. I felt my heart drop. Very rarely was I left out of introductions and conversations, and it felt like she had avoided me on purpose. I tried to brush off my disappointment, but I couldn't get a handle on it. I was upset. I didn't want to start my first day out of town being an outcast.

I stood up and walked over to Rica. "So, you never did ask for my name," I said, hoping that this would provoke conversation. "I noticed that you introduced yourself to everyone except for me."

Though most people would apologize at that moment and begin the process of getting to know you, Rica just grinned. I could feel my anger boiling at this point. I was embarrassed. Everything about the woman's nonverbal language told me that she had purposely ousted me, and I didn't feel like I had done anything to deserve that kind of treatment.

"That wasn't on purpose," Rica replied. "We were getting ready to take off. I figured at that point that names and such could wait until later."

I wanted to believe her, but something about her demeanor made me think that she was being facetious. I didn't know what I had done to her. I hadn't even spoken to Rica at this point, and already, she had something against me. Knowing this, I wondered if Rica had taken one look at me and judged me by my appearance. Women had done that in the past, and when they did that, it irritated me. Some people thought

I was just an entitled rich person that got what I wanted when I wanted it. If only they knew the truth. I worked hard for everything that I had gotten. I did my best not to rely on my parents' money, and I was determined to do things on my own. I wasn't some plastic doll that got everything paid for.

"My name, you mean?" I asked, calling Rica out on how she had treated me. I wasn't going to be singled out.

"What is it that you want me to do?" Rica shot back. It was obvious that she didn't feel sorry. She could have just introduced herself and moved on, but she was being stubborn.

"I want you to treat me the same way that you did everyone else," I replied, looking at her in the eyes. I was trying my best to keep my composure. I wanted to cry. I had just left everything I knew to come on this trip, and already, I had someone that didn't like me.

"Fine," Rica said, holding out her hand. "My name is Rica. What is yours?"

"Penny," I said. I didn't give her the benefit of shaking my hand. At this point, she had been clear about her intentions. She had wanted to leave me out.

The two of us parted, and I went back to my seat. My emotions were flowing wildly through my body at this point, and I started to wonder how the rest of the trip would go. I wasn't going to spend my entire time at this internship being excluded.

Chapter Fourteen

I spent most of the shuttle ride trying to calm down after my encounter with Rica. Even though the other woman was somewhat attractive...if that was even a thing one would think about a female...I wasn't going to lower my standards enough to give in to her rude behavior. I decided that instead of focusing on her, I would do my best to try to get to know the other women in the internship program. As far as I could tell, there were two other interns and four women that led the program, so even if I didn't get along with Rica, I would still have someone to talk to.

The shuttle finally stopped, and the University of San Francisco campus came into view. The campus looked large and beautiful. And I was excited to get off the shuttle and find out what our housing would be like. I had figured that since it was an internship program, we would probably be housed in a sorority house or possibly get vouchers so we could have our own apartments. Since this was a business program, I didn't doubt that they had funding to cover either of those situations, and I felt that the program leaders would want us each to have our own private housing so we could get used to our new work schedules without disturbing anyone else.

"Here we are," Brittney, the woman that had helped me with my bags earlier said.

"Brittney, are we going to be staying in the dorms?" a woman named Natalie asked. I had seen Natalie earlier when Rica had introduced herself to her. Natalie had said she was from Texas, and she had an easygoing attitude about her from what I had witnessed in conversation.

"Yes, the dorms that you will be in have been cleared out for the summer," Brittney responded. "There will still be college students in the other dorms on your floor due to summer classes, but we made sure there were enough rooms for the four of you."

"Dorm living," I commented. "This will definitely be an interesting experience."

I had never lived in a dorm before, and I had never planned to. I wasn't fond of the cramped quarters. I liked to have my own space and I also liked to have a bathroom and sink close to my room. I didn't like the idea of sharing a bathroom with dozens of other people. I didn't want to shower in a public stall. I wanted a nice, clean bathroom that wasn't used by anyone but me with a large bathtub and working shower.

But now it looked like I would be living in a small room near mutual shower and restroom facilities. I wouldn't have much privacy, because there would be people walking up and down the halls at all hours of the night. If someone decided to party, then I was at risk for missing sleep. I didn't like this at all. Not everyone had the same standards that I did when it came to keeping things clean. I could just picture myself coming down with some weird disease due to having to share quarters.

I sighed. I had been so excited about this internship. I had pictured myself staying in a nice place, starting a new career, and meeting a lot of new people that I could spend my free time with. However, since I had started on this journey, nothing had been up to my expectations. In fact, it seemed like most of the other candidates were young and inexperienced, and I was going to have to work with them while trying to get used to living like a freshman in a stinky dorm.

Chapter Fifteen

"Alright, ladies," the program leader said. Her name was Braelynn, and despite being disappointed about the other candidate's inexperience, I was impressed by her. I loved her business manner. She was eloquent when she spoke and she knew exactly what we were doing and when we were going to do it.

Knowing that there was someone that was prepared in this program calmed my nerves. I liked schedules. I liked knowing what the next step was. I liked being productive. I couldn't handle working with a whole bunch of people that were looking around, trying to figure out what to do next.

"Get your bags," Braelynn called. "We have a bit of a walk ahead of us."

I looked out the window. If we had to walk all the way to the dorms, I wasn't sure that I would be able to make it. I had packed quite a few bags in order to prepare for this trip, and I wasn't exactly used to bootcamping it across campus, especially in heels. I sighed.

"Walk?" I asked, hoping that there was some other option. Maybe, they had a golf cart or something that I could borrow just so I could get my bags where they needed to go. "I brought like three bags," I said, hoping someone would find a way to make this trip easier.

"Well, you can always go back to the shuttle and get whatever you can't carry," Rica snickered.

I shook my head. I was about tired of her. She was making it obvious that she wanted this experience to be a horrible one for me.

"We can help you," Christina replied, waving Brittney over.

"Yeah, we don't mind," Brittney said. "That's what we are here for."

"Thank you," I said, exasperated. "You gals have been so helpful. I don't know how I'm going to repay you."

"It's on the house," Christina said with a smile. "But only this once."

I laughed at her joke and walked with her and Brittney as we headed up to the dorms. The two of them had been extremely helpful, and they made me feel more welcome in this new city. I appreciated the fact that they opened me with welcoming arms, and after looking the two of them over, I wondered if we could be friends.

Brittney and Christina both dressed like I did, and they seemed to care about their manners. Even though I hadn't had much of a chance to converse with either of them, I could tell that we had things in common, and I appreciated this observation, because I had began to feel like I was somewhere I didn't belong.

The walk to the dorms was long, and by the time that we got there, I was out of breath. I leaned my hand against the brick building, preparing for a possible walk upstairs.

"Are you okay?" Brittney asked, coming up to me.

"Fine," I said. "I just didn't expect such a long walk. If I had, I would have worn my sneakers."

"Yeah, it's a bit of a jaunt in heels," Brittney said with a smile. "I've done it a time or two. It wasn't fun."

I looked at Brittney and smiled back. "Thank you again for helping me," I said.

"Not a problem," Brittney replied. "Let's get inside. We need to find out what dorm you are assigned to. We all will be meeting back up for lunch soon. You might want to change into more comfortable shoes before then."

"Oh, I will," I replied. "I have the perfect outfit for lunch. Just you wait."

Chapter Sixteen

I walked into the dormitory hall, looking around at the common area. It was quaint. There were a few spaces for people to talk and a few for people to study. It kind of reminded me of a small coffee shop. There wasn't exactly anything extraordinary about it. It seemed like the university was checking off boxes when they made the space. Nevertheless, the few people that occupied it seemed happy with the area, so I figured I wouldn't completely knock it. Though the common area wasn't my cup of tea, it obviously was just fine for other people.

I turned my attention towards the group. Braelynn was leading everyone up the stairs and onto the second floor. We followed her down a long hallway with blue-gray carpet, and she stopped in front of two rooms, opening the doors with the keys that she had brought with her. "These are the rooms that the university was willing to provide us for our program," she told us. "There are only two, so you ladies will have to double up."

I groaned internally. I knew that I would be sharing a bathroom and a shower, but now, I had to share a bedroom too. I wasn't the kind of person that liked to share my living quarters with anyone. I already had issues doing that with Rosita and Henry. Now, I was going to have to share my bedroom with some woman that I didn't even know. It made me cringe. Who knew what their hygiene habits would be like? What if they were messy? What if they were the type of person that never did laundry? It was clear that I wouldn't be able to invite anyone back to the dorms if I decided to network while I was on campus.

I looked over at the three other women that were in the internship program. I was either going to be roomed up with Rica, who didn't like me, Darla, who didn't talk, or Natalie, who I really didn't mind that much. Braelynn lifted the clipboard in her hand, scanning a sheet of paper with her eyes. Whatever she said next would one of the determining factors on how this program would go for me.

"I have assigned you to rooms," Braelynn said. "Rica, you will be rooming with Darla. You guys can take this room." Braelynn gestured to their room, and the two women turned to look at it.

I let out a breath. I wasn't going to be roomed with the mouthy one or the quiet one. I had gotten Natalie. She was the only one left. Braelynn pointed us towards our room and we both entered, checking out the place that we would be spending the next three months in.

"Ladies, get unpacked," Braelynn said. "You have a half an hour. After that, I want you to meet me in the cafeteria for lunch." She gave us each a folder that contained a campus map and our ID badge, and then she took off.

"I guess we can get comfortable for a while," I suggested to Natalie.

"That sounds nice," Natalie replied. "That plane ride took a lot out of me."

"I concur," I said, placing one of my bags on the chair near the desk. I didn't want any of the airport germs to get on my mattress. In fact, I needed to make sure that my mattress was clean in the first place. I took a pack of antibacterial wipes out of my bag and started wiping down my bed.

Natalie looked at me in confusion.

"You can never be too clean," I replied with a shrug. "Want one?"

Natalie shrugged back and took a wipe. "Sure," she said. "I never thought about packing these."

Chapter Seventeen

"Those really do work," Natalie said, turning around to show me her antibacterial wipe.

It was covered in dirt and grime, which made the thought of sleeping in the dorm seem disgusting. "Yeah, they are caked in dirt," I replied, showing her mine. "We are definitely going to have to pick up some antibacterial spray, so we can get this room cleaned up.

"And a trash can," Natalie said. "I really don't want to start messing this place up by discarding trash around the room."

"I agree with that," I said, going over to one of my bags and opening it. "As it turns out, I brought a small trash can." I pulled the small canister out of my bag, removing the contents that I had packed inside of it. I knew that I would have to bring what I needed, and though most people might not think about bringing items like a trash can, trash bags, and cleaning supplies, I had.

"Wow," Natalie replied, eyes wide. "I'm so glad you came prepared."

"Me too," I said, looking around the room. "I thought they would put us up in an apartment or at least one of the sorority houses. I didn't expect to have to live in a dorm."

"I don't mind the dorm too much," Natalie said. "At home, I only have my brother to keep me company. It might be nice to be close to people. That way, if we want to go out and do something or just have a conversation once in a while, we don't have to go far."

"I suppose," I said. "How long have you lived with your brother?"

"For years," Natalie said. "We went through foster care when we were younger, so we are very close."

I smiled at her. Looking at how put together she was, I would have never thought that she had endured a hard life. "It sounds like the two of you went through a lot."

"We did," Natalie said. "But you can't pick your life. You can only pick the choices that you make in it. That's why I am here. I want to make a better life for me and my brother. It's the least I can do. He's helped me with pretty much everything else. Do you have siblings?"

"No," I said with a smile. I could remember asking my mother for a brother or sister when I was very young. I always saw all of the other kids, playing with their siblings. They never seemed lonely or bored. My mother told me that she didn't want to have any more kids. She said that she was blessed with one, and that was enough for her to handle. I didn't understand what she meant by that until I was much older.

Apparently, I was a surprise to both of my parents. I wasn't planned. In fact, both of my parents told me that they had planned to work on their careers instead of starting a family. When my mother got pregnant and told my father, both of them were stunned. They rearranged their entire life plan to take care of me while maintaining their occupational lives. I wasn't sure whether to feel thankful for this or sad that they hadn't wanted me at first. I had mixed feelings, but it did appear that after I was born, both parents enjoyed having me around. Knowing this made me wonder how Natalie felt. Had she ever been anywhere where someone wanted her? How did she feel about her parents? What was her story? I didn't know the answers to any of these questions but I was determined to find out more.

Chapter Eighteen

"Okay," I said with a sigh. "I think this is the best that we can do until we get a wardrobe or something in here." I hung the outfits that I had unpacked and put hangers on on the side of the desk and looked over at Natalie.

"These are pretty tight quarters," she said with a laugh.

"Yeah, I don't know what we are going to do if either of us decides to go on a date," I replied. "It would just be too weird to bring the person back to the dorms."

"Well, you don't need to worry about that when it comes to me," Natalie said. "I don't date. I'm here to get as much knowledge as I can when it comes to this internship program. I don't have time for things like dating."

I laughed. "You sound like me," I said. "Even when I'm with someone, I feel that way. The last week that I spent with Henry drove me nuts. I couldn't get anything done, and I was happy when I finally got my own space."

"Who's Henry?" Natalie asked, putting her suitcase against the wall. "Was that your boyfriend?"

"Fiance," I replied. "We just broke up a couple of days before I got here."

"Dang," Natalie replied. "I'm sorry. What happened?"

"We just didn't mesh," I said. I wasn't used to giving out too much of my personal information, but Natalie was easy to talk to, and I didn't feel like she was using the information as a method to take advantage of me. "We went through the dating stage. We got to know each other, and we even lived together. But I never really felt like I connected with him. In fact, I've never really felt like I connected with anyone on a romantic level."

"Oh, wow," Natalie said. "And you lived with him? That must have been difficult. I don't think I could go through all that with someone that I wasn't in love with. For that matter, I couldn't even have sex with the person if I didn't have feelings for them."

I looked at Natalie. She didn't seem very experienced with dating. I could tell by her responses. "Have you ever been in a relationship with someone?" I asked her, curious to know the answer. I could understand her not wanting to date due to distrust since she had such a tumultuous childhood, but I had never met anyone that hadn't dated at all...except for maybe Rosita. I hadn't seen her with too many people or any people for that matter.

"No," Natalie said, her face getting red. "I'm just not interested," she replied. "My friend, Sharise has been trying to hook me up for years. The last time she tried to hook me up, I ended up going to a party with a gay guy."

"That's crazy," I said. "Didn't she know he was gay before she hooked the two of you up?"

"No," Natalie replied. "She has a habit of hooking me up with the friends of the guy she is interested in, but it never works out."

"Why?" I asked. "There had to be at least one guy that you had a good time with."

"No," Natalie said, clearly uncomfortable with the subject. "I don't like guys, so I never had that one guy that took my breath away or made me think twice. I'm attracted to women."

I looked at her closely, feeling slightly embarrassed. I wasn't really sure how to handle this situation. I looked down at my watch and back at her.

"Are you ready for lunch?" I asked, changing the subject.

"More than ready," Natalie said.

Chapter Nineteen

We were walking down the hall when I heard a familiar voice behind me. I turned around to see Rica and Darla trailing behind.

"What are you guys doing after lunch?" Rica asked us, like everything that happened before we got to the dorms was done and forgotten.

"Probably whatever the program leaders have planned," I said, not wanting to make plans with them after Rica had been so rude to me.

"Why?" Natalie asked. She was obviously intrigued. I couldn't blame her. Rica still looked hot even if she was an ass, and Natalie had said that she was into women. Maybe she was trying to pick her up. "What do you have in mind?"

"I want to go out," Rica said with a grin. "This is a nice city and there seems to be a lot to do."

What a slacker! She was already ready for a break, and the internship hadn't even started. I looked at those luscious black curls and her sarcastic brown eyes. I didn't understand what my body was doing at the moment, but I was getting irritated. Rica wasn't the best person when it came to staying motivated. She seemed to think like this whole thing was one big joke.

"We aren't here to see the city," I told her. "We are here to learn. If they wanted us going out and having fun, they would have invited us here for a vacation. This is an academic program, and it is important that we take this seriously. They might send us back home if we clown around."

My intent was to scare her, but it didn't work. She just kept looking at me like my words didn't matter. I wasn't used to being looked at like that. Most people were at least respectful to me. I didn't understand what this woman was doing to me.

"I don't think they have anything planned today," Rica said. "They told us to take a load off and get comfortable."

"That doesn't mean partying and wandering off," I shot back. Rica didn't seem to be listening so I turned around and continued my walk to the cafeteria. As I did, images of her going out and flirting with other women filled my head. It made me angry. I really felt mindfucked at this point. I didn't even know the woman and she was already playing with my mind. What did all of this mean? Why was it even happening?

"Are you okay?" Natalie asked as we walked across campus.

"I think so," I replied. "Rica just burns me. I don't know why she gets to me the way she does, but it's driving me up the wall."

"I know you date guys normally," Natalie replied. "But did you ever consider that you might have a crush on her? I mean, I could definitely be wrong. I don't have any dating experience, but the way you were looking at her and the way you responded made me think that you were trying to be more than friendly with her and she basically shot you down."

"I am not into her," I replied. "I mean, yeah, she's attractive, and there is something about her that makes you want to get to know her. But she's not like anyone else that I have dated. I have a type. She doesn't exactly fit my criteria, and besides, she is a female."

"Well, maybe, the 'type' that you have been trying to find isn't the one that meshes with who you really are," Natalie suggested. "Maybe, you haven't found someone that you are attracted to in a romantic capacity because you are looking for everything but what will work."

"I don't know about that," I replied.

Natalie just shrugged. She was obviously trying to help, but I was sure that she was a little off on her conclusions. There was no way I was attracted to women in a romantic sense.

Chapter Twenty

We walked towards the cafeteria, talking about the internship and who we hoped we would get matched up with. I had looked at the map that we were provided earlier so I could plan out our route. I didn't want to chance being late or not even making it to the cafeteria due to being lost. I wanted to make a good impression. I knew from experience that sometimes the people that made the bad impressions were matched up with the crappier jobs, and I really needed to be matched up with someone that could help me with my clothing company or at least give me some pointers.

"What about Braelynn?" Natalie asked. "She doesn't seem too bad. She pretty much runs the show."

"Yeah, I do like her work ethic," I replied. "But I was thinking that I would rather be paired with Brittney or Christina. Both of them seem to have a great sense of fashion, and it would be better to work with someone that has a background in my interest."

"Fair enough," Natalie said. "I don't really have any direction, so I figure I will let what happens happen. Maybe, I'll figure out what I want to do by working at the internship. I'm not even sure what kind of job would fit me."

I looked over at her. I didn't understand people that didn't have a sense of direction with their life. It didn't make much sense. I was very goal-oriented, and I was used to coming up with different objectives that I could achieve throughout my day. I felt like it gave me a sense of purpose.

"You never know what you will learn in this type of setting," I responded. Though I didn't understand her lack of goals, I did like Natalie. She had been one of the only people that was nice to me since I got to campus, and I didn't want to ruin our blooming friendship over something as petty as career goal differences.

"You're probably right about that," Natalie said. "I've always been good when it comes to school, but there's always a set itinerary. Here it seems like they give you the basic plan and you have to come up with the next steps."

"We'll see," I said. "Here," I said, opening the door to the cafeteria. "Let's get some of those questions answered."

We walked inside and I scanned the large room for the internship program leaders. Finally, I spotted them at a table in the back of the cafeteria. I led the way, noticing that Rica and Darla had arrived as well. Walking over to the table, I saw Brittney wave, and I waved back.

"Hello," I said, greeting all four women.

"Hi," Braelynn said. "Did you guys get something to eat?"

"No," Rica replied, before any of us could answer. "We weren't sure how to pay for our food. I know it's included in the program, but we didn't get vouchers or coupons or anything to scan."

I was embarrassed at this point. I knew how to get our food. I had read the packet. I was just under the impression that we should meet up with the leaders to show them that we had arrived before attempting to get our food. It was clear that Rica hadn't read anything, and now we were all going to look stupid for not being prepared.

"You have to use the temporary ID badge that we gave you," Braelynn replied. "They scan it when you check-out, and it will pay for your meal."

She looked irritated at this point, and I couldn't blame her. She probably thought that if we were motivated enough to apply for the internship, we should be motivated enough to read the material given to us. I could feel my face turn red. So much for first impressions.

"Okay," Rica said. "Then, I suppose we will go get our food and get back."

Chapter Twenty-One

I went to get my food. There was nothing that I could say to Braelynn at this point that would make up for how unprepared Rica had made us all look. I shook my head. Was I the only person that had read the packet? No. I guess Natalie had read it too, but that was mostly because we went over it together. Why hadn't Rica read it?

I looked over at the other woman. She was piling food on her tray like she hadn't eaten in months. How grotesque! Didn't she have any manners? Why would she want to make such a bad impression? Maybe, she didn't even care about the internship. Maybe she had gotten the opportunity and thought of it as a free trip out of town. Rica made me so mad. She was making us all look unprepared just because she didn't care. I wasn't going to let her take me down like that.

I focused on my food. I got a salad and some fruit. I didn't want to get anything that would create a mess. I was wearing nice clothes, and I didn't want to spill on myself and look like a slob. I walked back to the table and sat down, waiting for the other interns to get back as well.

"So, how do you like it so far," Brittany asked me after I got seated.

"I haven't gotten too much of a chance to explore the campus, but it looks nice," I replied. "I'm trying to get used to the dorms. I haven't lived with anyone besides my ex and my best friend for years, so it is a little different trying to live in a place where people are constantly walking down halls and you have to share a bathroom."

"I can understand," Brittany replied. "It would be different to go from being on your own to cohabitating with a bunch of women, but give it some time. It might be a fun experience. Some of my best memories come from dorm living, and it's not as bad as you might think it would be."

I nodded. Maybe she was right. I didn't mind sharing my space with Natalie. I might be able to get used to having someone to come home to and talk to. When I lived with Henry, our schedules were drastically different, so I didn't really have much of a chance to tell him about my day. Living with Rosita was somewhat similar. She worked late, so by the time we had a chance to talk, it was almost time for bed.

At that moment, Natalie, Darla, and Rica got back to the table. They set down their trays and Braelynn pulled out a folder and handed the other leaders a piece of paper. "Alright, now that you are settled in, it's time to get to business," Braelynn said, addressing all of the interns. "Each of you will be shadowing one of us. We all help run a separate business in the San Francisco area, and you will be able to follow us during our day to day operations so you can learn how to run a business and how to deal with certain barriers that you might come across."

"How do we know who we are paired with?" I asked, looking at each of the leaders.

I knew that the person that they matched me up with would help determine how successful I would be in the clothing industry. There was a chance that I would be paired with someone that worked in an entirely different type of work, and though I still might be able to learn how to deal with the regular business processes that all companies have to deal with like inventory, billing, etc., I wouldn't be able to see how those skills were specific to my type of work. I took a deep breath and waited for Braelynn to tell us who we were matched with. I sure hoped it was someone that could help me go further in fashion.

Chapter Twenty-Two

"I have the list right here," Braelynn said, looking back at me. "Penny, you will be working with Brittney. Brittney runs a sustainable clothing brand."

I was beaming at this point. Brittney had been so nice. She had helped me carry my bags up to the dorms, and she had been very encouraging when it came to the transition to California. "That's right up my alley," I replied, smiling.

"I love your enthusiasm," Brittney commented. "I don't think we will have an issue getting along."

I smiled back at Brittney. She seemed to have a good heart, and I was sure that she would be able to teach me more about running a clothing company than I already knew. Focus was turned towards the other internship participants as they were matched up with their program leaders, and quietly celebrated my successful match while Braelynn continued with her conversation.

I felt blessed to have been matched with a person that not only worked in the same industry that I did but also was easy to get along with. I had been worried about getting placed with a leader whose personality type didn't match mine. I looked over at Brittney, who had turned her attention to her friend Christina. Christina looked back at her, fully attentive, and I paid attention to how they interacted.

I could tell from the get go that they were best friends, but the nonverbal language that I picked up on between them said a lot more. They sat very close to each other and they were comfortable touching each other on the shoulders, arms, and legs. There were a couple of times where Christina wrapped her arm around Brittney's shoulders, and the way they looked at each other when they talked, made it clear that they didn't have to verbalize all of their conversation.

Watching them together made me wonder if they were a couple. It had never crossed my mind that Brittney might be lesbian, but after watching how she interacted with her best friend, the thought was there.

When I came to California, I had expected to meet more liberal people than I knew back home. I thought that I would come across women that liked to wear loose clothing and smoke things that I didn't quite agree with. However, I never thought that I would meet as many gay people as I had. It was clear that Rica was gay, and Natalie had told me earlier that she was gay. Now, after watching Christina and Brittney talking to each other, I was sure that they were gay too.

I wasn't sure if this bothered me or not. I didn't really have gay friends. It just wasn't my world. I wasn't against people falling in love with the person that they meshed with, but I also didn't like the idea that one of these women might hit on me. It made me feel a little uncomfortable. I mean, I was pretty hot if I did say so myself, and I had a good educational record and ran my own business. I was quite a catch, so it would be odd if they didn't go for me. The problem was that I wasn't gay, or at least I didn't think so. I had been taken with Rica when we first arrived, but that could have just been because of her personality. I shook my head. I was confused. I was among people that I didn't fully understand, and I hoped that we would all be able to focus more on our careers than our love lives, because I didn't think I was ready for all this.

Chapter Twenty-Three

"Before you leave, I'd like to talk to you," Brittney called to me from across the table.

"Okay," I said. "I'm going to dump my tray, and I'll be back."

"I'll wait for you by the door," Natalie said, tapping me on the shoulder as I got up to dump my tray.

"Alright," I replied. I was happy that she was willing to wait. I still wasn't familiar with this campus, and it would be nice to have company while I walked back to the dorms.

I went over to the trash and dumped my tray, wondering what Brittney wanted to go over. Though I was sure that I had picked up on the fact that she was gay, I still did like Brittney. She was nice, and I wasn't willing to let her love life get in the way of what she had to teach me as long as we kept our relationship professional.

I walked back to the table that we were sitting at. Brittney was the only one sitting there. Everyone else had gone their separate ways. I sat down across from the other woman and waited for her to speak.

"So, I wanted to give you more information on this internship," Brittney said as soon as I was seated. "I usually go to work at 5 a.m., but I don't expect you to be there that early. I think it would be alright if you arrived at seven."

"Okay," I replied. "But if you want me to be there at five as well, I don't mind."

"That's kind of early," she said. "I don't want to tire you out before we even start."

"I really don't mind," I told her. "I came here to work. I didn't expect to do anything else."

"Okay," Brittney said, looking at me closely. "Then, come at five. Here's the address." She handed me a small piece of paper and I took it from her hand. "You can either take the bus there, or you can call a taxi. I would take the bus though. It is a lot cheaper."

"Sounds good to me," I said.

"Now, we will be working with other students from the fashion program at the university," Brittney continued. "They are working to complete their internship hours, so they are not paid a financial compensation."

"I see," I replied. "So, this internship is unpaid."

"No," Brittney said. "You will get a paycheck. See, the thing is I'm looking for an assistant manager for my business, and I really would like to test you out to see if you fit the criteria. If you do a good job while you are in this program, then I might be able to offer you a full-time position."

"Really?" I asked. I felt all kinds of emotions flow through me. If I got a full-time position with her, then I would be able to work in the fashion industry and make a steady paycheck. However, it would also mean that I would have to close my own business. It was a toss-up. My business hadn't been making the money that I needed it to, but her business clearly was. So, if she offered me the position at her company, I would have a big decision to make. I would either have to close my business so I could work for hers, or I would have to turn her down and hope that I could get my business out of the hole. That was a life-changing decision to make, and I wasn't really sure what my choice would be. Maybe I would figure it out over time.

Chapter Twenty-Four

"Wow, that took a long time," Natalie said as I came to the door. "What did she talk to you about? Is everything okay?"

"It's more than okay," I said. "She said that if I do really well, I might have a full-time position here in San Francisco."

"That's great," Natalie said, giving me a hug. "You are so organized, and out of all of us, you are probably the most prepared. I hope you get it."

"Me too," I said with a smile. It was great to have the opportunity, but it was even better to have someone excited for me. Usually, my friends expected me to do well, and when I didn't, they were disappointed. Natalie was different. She was genuinely happy that I had a chance at getting a job that paid well in my dream career field.

"So, is she going to train you, or how does it all work?" Natalie asked.

"She is going to show me the ropes, and then, she is going to slowly transition me into the assistant manager role," I said. "I'm happy to have the opportunity, but it makes me wonder if I'm a failure when it comes to my own business. You see, I would have to close my business in order to take up this job."

"Maybe, the two of you can collaborate," Natalie suggested. "It seems like Brittney is looking for a new approach at running her business. Maybe if you show her what you already have going, she will be able to build on it. Then, you can have your business and be the assistant manager for her company."

"That's not a bad idea," I said, contemplating this new plan. "It would be like having a co-owner, and in essence, that might make me a co-owner of her business, which would result in a larger compensation."

"Well, yeah, but slow your roll," Natalie said. "You still need to talk to her about doing all that, and she still needs to agree to it."

"True," I replied. "And some people aren't too keen on sharing the spotlight when it comes to running a business."

"But it doesn't hurt to ask," Natalie added. "And if it works out, then both of you might be able to further your success in the fashion world without having to give up any of your own ideas."

"You know, you're pretty smart," I told Natalie as we walked down the sidewalk that led to the dorms.

"Well, thanks," she said. "I do my best."

"So, how did your talk with Christina go?" I asked her. "When do you have to be at work?"

"I can't say that my experience went as well as yours did," Natalie replied. "Christina is definitely an a-type personality, and she seems to be worried that I will mess up before I even begin."

"Dang," I replied. I had hoped that she would have had a similar experience to mine. Natalie was so easy to get along with, and I couldn't see her having conflict with anyone, especially in a business environment.

"It'll be okay," Natalie said. "She is just probably nervous. Maybe after we start working together, she will see that she made the right decision. I don't blame her for wanting to see what she signed up for."

"Is she at least going to pay you for your work?" I inquired.

"Yes," Natalie said. "I will get paid minimum wage. She is going to give me the chance to work my way up to a bigger position, but she is very serious about things being on point. So, I need to make sure that I make it to work on time tomorrow."

"Did she give you the address?" I asked.

"No," Natalie said with a smile. "She gave me the name of the business, and she told me that I could look it up online and GPS it. So, I will be spending my night, trying to figure out how to get to work."

I shook my head. It was crazy how different Brittney and Christina were. I had thought with them being best friends that they would have similar attitudes, but that wasn't the case.

Chapter Twenty-Five

"**A**re you still trying to figure out how to get to work?" I asked Natalie.

We had been back at the dorms for a couple of hours at this point, and she had spent most of the time writing bus routes down in a notebook that she had brought with her.

"I am," Natalie said. "I just want to make sure that there is more than one way to get there. What if one of the buses closes down for the day? What if there is a traffic slowdown? I want to make sure that I leave myself enough options."

"Calm down," I said. Hearing myself say this was weird. Usually, I was the one freaking out about being late. "You'll be fine. You need to take some time to relax, because as soon as we start these internships, we probably won't have much free time."

"True," Natalie said with a sigh. "I'm just usually on top of these things, and the way Christina was talking to me made me feel like she didn't trust that I could fulfill my responsibilities."

"She is probably just as nervous as you are about this process," I said. "Can you imagine recruiting a stranger to work at a business that you spent so much time building? And to work in a restaurant at that? Christina probably wants to make it clear that she is serious about what she expects out of you. I don't think she is trying to scare you away. She has probably had workers in the past that did the bare minimum, and with her schedule, she might not be able to afford to hire someone that can't follow the guidelines that she set for them."

"I can understand that," Natalie said. "I just don't want to let her down. I'm used to being good at this kind of stuff. I've never had anyone make it clear to me that they weren't sure that I could keep up with a task that I signed up to do...unless it had something to do with dating. I'll never be able to keep up with that."

I laughed. "Well, at least you don't have to focus on that while you are here," I said. "Keep your eye on the ball. Do what you can to be prepared, and try to relax. You don't want to start your first day a nervous mess. That's not a good impression to make either."

Natalie looked at me and nodded. "You're probably right," she said. "Maybe, I'll read a book or something. I do need to get my mind off this process for a minute. If I don't, I'll go nuts."

"Okay, well you do that, and I'm going to go to the athletic complex," I said.

"What do you need from there?" Natalie asked, interested.

I smiled. "I was so worried about having to take a shower in the dorms that Brittney told me about the showers in the athletic complex," I replied. "She said that during this time of year, the building was mostly empty, and since the athletic department has a lot of funding, they have a cleaning company go in there and clean the bathrooms twice a day. I figured that I would give them a try. The bathrooms here look gross. The last time I looked around, someone left their retainer in one of the sinks."

"Let me know if she's right," Natalie replied. "I wouldn't mind using a cleaner shower. I'm used to Trent's goobers in the bathroom, but I don't really want to deal with the messes of all the other people on this floor."

"No kidding," I said. "Well, when I come back, I will let you know how it worked out. I'm going to leave my purse and key here if you are just going to stay in the dorms. Is that okay?"

"Yeah, that should be fine," Natalie said. "You might want to take your phone though."

"I will," I said. "You can never be too safe." I grabbed a dress, some underwear, a towel, a hair brush, and a new pair of heels. Just because I was getting prepared to settle down for the night didn't mean that I had to walk across campus looking like it.

Chapter Twenty-Six

I started walking across campus and towards the athletic complex. I was happy that Brittney had told me about the showers there. I was looking forward to a hot, quiet shower without having to be bothered by the hustling and bustling of the dorms. I neared the complex and walked in. It seemed quiet besides the few weightlifters that were walking about.

I looked for a sign for the lockers and found one on the side of the weightlifting room. Walking in, I looked around for a place to set my clean outfit and hairbrush. Everything in the lockers looked spotless, so I decided to forgo putting these items in a locker and just set them down on a nearby bench. I walked into a shower stall and set my towel and heels in there. Then, I walked around to the bathroom stalls so I could pee before I showered.

I pulled the door shut, but for some reason, it kept bouncing back open. It appeared that the lock was broken. I pulled harder. Maybe, it would still close if I could stick it shut. Boom! The door shut and I could feel my flip flop slip on something wet on the floor. I fell backwards into the wall, and my hair got tangled in something sticky on the wall. Pulling my head off the wall, I saw a long string of gum string its way from the wall to my hair. Yuck! Apparently, the cleaning crew hadn't touched on the bathroom yet.

I did my best to untangle my hair from the sticky gum and sat down on the toilet. I had to pee. I wiped and got up, adjusting myself. My flip flop was covered in the wet substance on the floor, so I decided to dispose of both of them. What was one flip flop going to do? I flushed the toilet and tried to push myself out of the stall, but it was stuck. I had stuck it so hard that it wouldn't open.

I pushed hard, but before I could get a good enough grip on the door, I felt something wet running over my feet. The toilet was overflowing, and worse than that, water was spraying from the pipe on the back of the toilet. I was covered in toilet water. I pushed and pushed until the bathroom door opened and finally it did, sending me flying across the locker room floor. I was a mess.

I got up off the floor. I stunk! I couldn't go anywhere like this. Hopefully, the shower would help. I took off my wet clothing, throwing them in the trash as well. There was no point in keeping them. Who knew what kind of germs were on them by now? I went into the shower stall that I had left my towel in and turned on the water. Feeling the hot water run over my back felt good, especially after being covered in toilet water. I reached for my soap bottle, but I couldn't find it. I wiped my eyes with my hands and looked around. I had forgotten my soap bottle! Great! Now, I was just wet and dirty.

I turned off the shower and dried off with my towel, making my way back into the locker. This time, I wasn't alone. There were a few women in there changing out of softball outfits. I did my best to comb my hair and put on my clothing as fast as I could. Just as I was about to leave the locker room, I realized that I forgot my heels. I put my towel and brush on the bench and went back to the shower stall to get my heels, but someone was already in there. This entire experience had been horrible at this point, but there was no way I was going to leave my shoes behind.

Chapter Twenty-Seven

I didn't know how I was going to get my heels, but I was bound and determined not to leave them behind. I tried tapping on the shower curtain and calling to the woman that was in there, but there was no answer. Then, I stepped back so I could look at the bottom of the shower to see if there was a way for me to reach under there without disturbing the woman. There wasn't. If I did that, she would probably think that I was trying to get a peep show, and I certainly didn't want to send that message.

"What's wrong?" a bulky brunette asked. She was still changing out of her softball uniform, and apparently, I had caught her eye.

"I left my shoes in there," I said. "And they are designer heels, so I don't want to leave without them."

"Designer huh?" the brunette asked with a laugh.

"Yes," I said, somewhat offended. If only she understood what I had to do to get them then she wouldn't think it was such a joke.

"Hey, Lara," the brunette called.

"Yeah," a voice called from the shower.

"Barbie lost her heels in your shower," the brunette replied. "Can you toss them over?"

"No problem," Lara said. "This isn't the first time that I've had that happen."

The brunette laughed, and the woman in the shower dangled my heels out of the shower, and I grabbed them.

"Thanks," I said, rushing out of the locker room. That brunette had pissed me off. Not only had she been rude by calling me Barbie, but she continued to laugh at me. I didn't know her from shit. Why did she think that she could treat me that way? I walked out of the athletic complex and down the sidewalks towards the dorm. I was ready to get back to a safe space where people weren't hassling me.

As I walked down the sidewalk, two familiar people caught my eyes. Darla and Rica were walking towards me. Of course, they had to show up after the situation that I had been through. It was like they knew when I was having issues and had to show up so they could make it worse. I tried to get my composure. I didn't want them to see me taken off guard.

"Hi, guys," I said, trying to be nice. Maybe if I was nice, they wouldn't make my night worse. "What are you doing out so late?"

"I'd like to ask you the same thing, Rica said, looking me up and down.

I blushed. I was hardly put together, and I could feel her eyes warm every part of my body that she looked at. "Your outfit looks lovely. It's a shame I didn't see it earlier."

My heart started beating a mile a minute, and I felt like I couldn't catch my breath. Rica was looking at me! Why now? I wasn't prepared for this. I didn't put on my make-up. I wasn't even wearing one of my best outfits. "I just bought it," I said. "In fact, I took the time to find an outfit that would work with my internship."

I don't know why I felt the need to lie...maybe, so she didn't think I was wearing last season's formal. I don't know. I just didn't want to let her know what I had really been through. I'm sure she would think it was gross if she knew about the toilet exploding all over me and the fact that I hadn't gotten to wash with soap. I didn't want Rica to think I was gross. I wanted her to see me when I was looking good, but right now wasn't one of those moments, and I really wanted to run away far from her and Darla until I could get myself put together.

"Where's your bag?" Darla asked me.

I was getting irritated. Why wouldn't they just let me go on my way? "I don't have a bag," I said. "I liked the dress so much that I wore it out of the store." By now, I wasn't even keeping track of the lies I was telling. I was just trying to escape.

"Where are the clothes you were wearing when you went shopping?" Rica asked.

"I threw them away," I said quickly. "Now, if the two of you would leave me alone, I have somewhere I need to be."

"Alright, see you later," Rica said. "Be careful in those heels."

"Thanks," I said, glad to see them leaving. I needed a real shower and I needed to get into a fresh outfit. I felt gross.

Chapter Twenty-Eight

I got to the dormitory building and rushed up the stairs, but in the process, my heel broke. I was left hobbling down the hallway without shoes. Now, not only was I covered in toilet water but I had whatever dirt was on the carpet on my feet. I got to my dorm room and I knocked on the door. Natalie answered.

"That was quick," she said, letting me in. "What's that smell?"

I blushed and instantly started to cry. I told her about what had happened at the athletic complex and how I ended up running into Darla and Rica on the way back. I was so upset at this moment that I wanted to bury myself under my covers, but I was too dirty to even sit in a chair.

"You'll be okay," Natalie said. "Go take a shower here. Maybe, Brittney was wrong. Maybe, the athletic complex wasn't the best place to go."

"Maybe," I said. I didn't want to argue. I just wanted to get clean.

"Here," Natalie said, digging through her bag until she had a bottle of soap in her hand. "Use this. Do you have a towel?"

"I did," I said. "I think I left that and my hair brush at the athletic complex with my phone. Hopefully, they are still there."

"Hopefully," Natalie replied, surprised. "How about you go shower, and when you get done, we can walk down there together and get your stuff?"

"Alright," I said.

"I have an extra towel if you need it," Natalie offered.

"That's okay," I said, pulling a towel from my pile of clothes. "I brought a couple. That whole toilet issue just knocked me off my game."

"I think that would knock anyone off their game," Natalie replied. "I can't believe you had so many issues."

"Neither can I," I said. "And on the day before my internship. Hopefully, everything will straighten itself out."

"It might," Natalie said. "But you have to move forward. There's no point in dwelling on what happened. It's already said and done. Now, you need to focus on what you need to do to be prepared for tomorrow, and the first thing that you probably need to do is to wash that toilet water off of yourself."

I laughed. "It is pretty stinky, isn't it?"

"Yeah, when you came up to the door, I thought that a pipe had broken in the building," Natalie said. "I didn't even hear you knock. I came to the door to find out what was going on."

"I smell that bad?" I asked, almost back to tears.

Natalie looked at me compassionately. "If it makes you feel better, your hair looks nice."

I smiled. I wanted to hug her, but I didn't want her to get dirty from everything that I was covered in.

"Go take your shower," Natalie urged.

I nodded and grabbed my shower gear. I needed to start focusing on what I could do from this point on. She was right. There was no reason to focus on the past. If I was going to do good at this internship, I needed to get myself together.

I walked out of the door and into the dorm bathroom. It was empty, and though it wasn't the cleanest, it also didn't smell like sewage. I had brought a clean outfit and a new pair of flip flops and I started to get undressed. At least this time I had soap, and I had a clean towel. Maybe, I would feel better after I smelled less like sewage and more like my normal self.

Chapter Twenty-Nine

I got done with my shower and walked back to the dorm room, happy to be clean and free from toilet debris. When I got to the room, I noticed Natalie just sitting there with a smile on her face.

"Are you okay?" I asked, hoping this wasn't some weird mental breakdown due to the stress of the internship. Though I should really be the one breaking down, I still wanted to be cautious while around the other interns. You never knew when someone was going to crack.

"I'm fine," Natalie said with a laugh. "I was listening to the music."

"What music?" I asked, giving her a look.

"Listen," she said, putting a finger to her mouth.

I stopped talking and stood still, trying to figure out what she was talking about. Then, I heard it too. There was definitely music playing somewhere down the hall. It made me wonder where it was coming from.

"Do you want to go check it out?" Natalie asked, hopping up from her bed.

I shrugged. "It's probably someone in the dorms enjoying their night."

"Well, don't you think that it's about time you enjoyed your night too?" Natalie inquired. "You already had to deal with Rica all day. You did everything that you need to do for the internship, and you had a toilet explode on you. I think it's about time, you had a little fun."

"Fun?" I joked. "What's that?"

"I'm going to show you," Natalie said, taking my hand and leading me to the door. "We have to live here for three months. We might as well get the true experience of living in the dorms."

I wanted to argue, but there was a part of me that agreed. I had already had to adjust to living with other people. The entire day had been stressful. Maybe, Natalie was right. Maybe, it was time to kick back and relax. It couldn't hurt. Besides, if I was in my own place, I would probably be enjoying a glass of wine right about now.

"Alright," I said as Natalie pulled me down the hall, towards the noise. "It's not like we have anything else to do."

Natalie walked further down the hall, stopping every so often so she could listen to the music, until she eventually found the source of the noise. She pressed her ear against the dorm room door of the room that the music was coming from and looked back at me. "I think we found a winner," she said.

Just as the words came out of her mouth, the door opened and a brown-eyed woman with curly hair appeared. "Did you get an invite?" she asked, looking at us skeptically.

"No," Natalie said with a shrug.

"They're good," a man with a buzz cut said, popping his head out the door as well. "Come on in, guys. We are celebrating Marcia's birthday. Are you from around here?"

"No," Natalie replied, walking through the door and beckoning for me to follow. "But just because we are from out of town, doesn't mean that we aren't happy for Marcia."

"It seems like everyone is happy for Marcia," I commented as I got into the room. There were people packed in the small room. A disco ball was turning on a nearby desk, and there were cases of beer everywhere. "Happy birthday, Marcia," I said, cracking open a bottle. I still didn't know who the other woman was, but I was happy to get the small reprieve from the internship experience. It really had been a long day, and maybe, Natalie was right. Maybe, I needed to chill out a little bit. After all, we were in college.

Chapter Thirty

I looked over and saw Natalie drinking out of a bottle of water. "Do you want one?" I asked, holding up the beer.

"No, thanks," she mouthed. "I'm not a big drinker."

I nodded. Usually, I wasn't a big drinker either. I liked to have wine from time to time, but besides that, I maintained a pretty sober lifestyle. However, today was a bit different. This was one of my first experiences at a dorm party, and I wanted to let loose and enjoy my time. It wasn't every day that I got invited to a party like this.

Usually, the parties that I attended were more formal. There was a dinner and horderves, and instead of music and disco lights, the evening was filled with conversation. It was nice, but it wasn't exactly the type of parties that others my age were enjoying. I heard all kinds of stories from people that went to the wild parties that I either wasn't invited to or wasn't allowed to go to. They made out with strangers, swam naked in the pools, and danced until the sun came back up. I had always wanted to go to a party like that. I just didn't have the nerve. Besides, I had a reputation to uphold back home, and if I was caught dead at one of those kinds of parties, it would probably cause damage.

"Are you having fun?" Natalie asked.

I nodded, placing my empty beer bottle on the desk. "Do you want to dance?"

Natalie looked at me apprehensively. It was obvious that she probably hadn't too much experience in that area. Therefore, instead of waiting for her response, I just took her hand in mine and pulled her close. She found her footing and her hands found their way to my waist. I could feel goosebumps erupt around the area that she was touching and my face started to get warm.

"Are you okay?" Natalie asked.

I could hear her now. She was close enough to me that we no longer had to mouth our sentences. "I'm good," I said, even though a range of things were happening to my body that I had no control over.

"Good," she said, pulling me closer.

I felt her hip caress mine and I instantly felt turned on. It was weird. I had never had sexual feelings for a woman, at least not ones that made my body react in the way in which it was now. Her stomach brushed up against mind and our breasts were nearly touching. I looked Natalie in the eyes, and she looked back at me and smiled. I wondered if she was feeling the same warm sensation run through her body. It was hard to tell. Natalie was probably used to the touch of a woman. She probably had all kinds of experience with this type of intimacy, and here I was, trying to figure out if the butterflies in my stomach had made their way between my legs.

"Careful," Natalie said as I briefly lost my step. She held me tight so I didn't fall, but as soon as she let go, I felt myself stumble again.

"Thank you," I said with a sheepish smile as she caught me. She was stronger than I had originally thought. I hadn't expected her to catch me like that, but then again, I also hadn't expected to fall.

Her muscular arms had made me feel so secure and when she pulled me up, I had fallen right into her chest. She didn't even budge. She had held me firmly in her arms until I was steady again.

I looked at Natalie closely. There was a definite chemistry in the air. She locked her eyes with mine and the two of us continued to dance, but this time, we were closer and there was an obvious spark.

Chapter Thirty-One

J ust as we got our groove, someone lowered the music and a man
called for silence. Everybody stopped dancing and looked at the
back of the room where the man was standing, holding a small
television. "Thank you for coming, everyone," he said. "My name is
Josh for those of you that don't know me, and I have been friends with
Marcia for a long time. In fact, the two of us go way back to
kindergarten. Anyway, I wanted to liven things up again. After all, it is
Marcia's twenty-first birthday, and you only get one chance to celebrate
a milestone like that, so if you guys can file into five lines, we are going
to have a knockout shot contest. The last person standing will win this
television in my hands."

"Come on," I said to Natalie, pulling her towards a line.

"I'm not drinking," she replied. "You have to take shots to win."

"Come on," I urged. "Just this once. I never go to parties like this.
This might be the only time in your life that you can say that you took
shots with me."

Natalie looked at my face and then nodded. "Fine," she said. "Just
tonight. I suppose I could blow off a little steam too. It doesn't look like
I will be having a lot of time in my schedule to do things like this while
I am out here."

"Right," I said, pulling her into one of the lines. "Besides, it might
be fun. We might win a television for our dorm."

"That would be nice," Natalie said. "I wonder if it has streaming
access."

"I don't know," I replied. "But I don't see why it wouldn't."

We got in our line and watched as a small table was placed in front
of the five lines. A woman laid down on it, exposing her stomach and
the man in the front poured liquor into her belly button. "First up," he
said and a person from the first line instantly went up to the woman
and slurped the liquor out of her belly button. I shivered. Not only was

I intimidated by the fact that I would have to put my mouth on another person, but I wasn't too enthused by slurping anything out of anyone's belly button.

"You're starting to regret it, aren't you?" Natalie asked me with a grin.

"No," I lied, looking at her with a stern expression. "I made a commitment. I'm going to go through with it."

"Commitment?" she laughed. "I didn't know that this qualified as a commitment."

"Well, we are in line, aren't we?" I replied. "If we got in line, we have to go through with it. Besides, after I get through the initial disgust, I'm pretty sure I will win."

"I didn't know you drank like that," Natalie said.

"I don't," I replied. "But I'm persistent. I don't think anyone else here will have the same motivation that I do."

"We'll see," Natalie replied. "I'm pretty persistent myself, especially when there is a television to be won."

I looked at the small television. I knew that I could easily buy one for myself, but the thought of earning it seemed more interesting. I looked over at Natalie. She appeared to be gearing herself up for a win. I shook my head. There was no way that she was going to beat me at this contest. She didn't even drink on a regular basis. There was a good chance she would be out by the fourth round.

"Ready?" Natalie asked, pointing to the front of the line. There was only one person in front of me.

"Ready as I'll ever be," I said.

Chapter Thirty-Two

I don't even know how many rounds of drinks we did before I saw Natalie back out and walk towards the door. I wasn't sure what she was doing, but I knew that I couldn't let her go by herself, so even though I really wanted to win the small television, I followed her. I figured in the long run, the television wasn't worth her safety, and I wasn't sure how intoxicated she was. She said that she didn't drink very often, and I knew that if I was feeling tipsy, she probably was too.

"You okay?" I asked as soon as both of us were in the hallway.

Natalie turned around and looked at me with a smile. "I'm a little drunk, but I'm okay," she replied. "You know, you don't have to follow me. I'll be just fine. I just want to go get a little air. It was really hot in that room."

I looked at her. She looked like she was telling me the truth, so I considered going back for the television. But somehow I had already lost interest in the small prize, and Natalie's idea of a walk actually sounded like a good idea. "I'll go with you," I said. "That is, if you want my company."

"Well, come on then," Natalie said, waving me along. "The weather was nice earlier. I bet it's cooled down a little, but I'm sure that it will be decent enough for a walk around."

I followed her in silence. It was kind of nice just being in her company. Natalie wasn't like the other women that I usually hung around. She was much calmer, and it didn't seem like there was a lot that bothered her.

We walked down the dorm stairs and out of the front door, finding a small path on the side of the dorms that looked like it was built to be a walking trail. "Well, this is nice," I said, feeling the cool breeze on my hot face.

"It sure is," Natalie said with a smile. "I didn't know how much longer I could stay in that room. It started to get hot and stuffy, and there were way too many people in one area."

I laughed. "You are not much of a partier are you?" I asked, looking at Natalie's simple attire.

"Not really," Natalie said. "It's just too much noise and chaos for me. Don't get me wrong. I do go to parties from time to time, but usually it's Sharise's idea to go, not mine."

"Sharise?" I asked. "That's your best friend back home right?"

"Yeah," Natalie replied. "We usually spend a lot of time together. She is always on a man hunt. I'm not sure anything else keeps her attention...well, maybe the mall...but besides that."

"What do you like to do when you aren't engaging in her plans?" I asked her. I had heard a lot about what Natalie did with her friend and her brother but not a lot about Natalie. I wondered if she was hiding who she was from me or if she really wasn't sure what to do without her loved ones.

"I like to read," Natalie said simply. "I like walks. I kind of just do things when they feel right. I feel like planning too many things takes some of the fun out of them, and I really never grew up being able to count on too much, so I try not to put myself in that position."

"I can understand that," I said, looking over at her face as it glinted in the moonlight. I wasn't sure if it was the quiet contentness that I felt when I was with her or the alcohol that was swimming through my body, but she looked attractive.

Chapter Thirty-Three

I looked at Natalie, and she looked back at me. For a moment, we were in our own quiet world, together and without a care. I felt myself get closer to her, and my lips rested on hers. She responded almost immediately, caressing her lips against mine and wrapping her arms around my body. She was gentle and her kisses her soft, not like the rough ones that I experienced with Henry when he was ready for some action.

Natalie took her time, her emotion in every caress and every kiss. I responded. It felt natural and it didn't have any of the pressure that I normally experienced when I was with a man. "Do you want to take this upstairs?" I asked. I could feel goosebumps erupting across my skin at this point, and wetness flowing out of my hot center.

"We can," Natalie said. "Are you sure that you are ready for that?"

"I'm more than ready," I said, taking her hand and pulling her back towards the dorms. "Come on. Let's go somewhere more comfortable."

I led her to the dorms and up the stairs. The dorm was quiet at this point besides the party that was occurring at the end of the hall. We walked into our room and closed the door, and as soon as the dorm was closed, I turned Natalie around and pinned her up against it, once again finding her lips. I kissed her deeply, curious to know more about her. I didn't know why she intrigued me so much. I wasn't sure if it was her personality or if it was her body, but I wanted to make sense of it all. She pulled off her shirt and I helped her with her bra and she did the same for me. We both shed our remaining clothing in a fit of ecstasy until we stood skin to skin. I pulled her up, until her legs were wrapped around my waist and her back was against the door. Then, I guided my fingers into the soft folds between her thighs and began to pump until I felt the muscles tighten around my fingers.

Natalie held onto me tightly, moaning with each motion and positioned one of her breasts parallel with my lips. I pulled her nipple into my mouth, softly moving my tongue around the exterior until the warmth between her legs was accompanied by a wet, warm fluid. I continued to kiss her breast as I doved my fingers deeper and deeper into the depths of her center. I could feel her body harden and I moved my lips towards hers, taking in a more intense kiss than before. With each movement, I felt her get closer until I finally felt her jerk back and moan so loudly that I was sure everyone in the dorm could hear it. I held her tightly and waited for her body to relax.

"Wow," she said between breaths. "Was that your first time?"

"With a woman," I replied.

"How did you know what to do?" she asked. "I have never had sex like that."

"I don't know," I said with a shrug. "I guess it just came naturally."

Natalie nodded and I helped her find her footing so we could lay down on the bed. "So, what does this mean?" she asked. "Does this make us a couple? Was this a one-night stand?"

"I haven't really thought about any of that," I replied. And I didn't want to think about it either. I just wanted to enjoy the moment and see where it went. I didn't even know if I was a lesbian or if I was bisexual or if this was just an experience.

Chapter Thirty-Four

An alarm filled the air, and I woke up right away. I looked around for the source of the noise, realizing that it was my phone and drew a blank as to why I had set it. I felt sore and tired, and I knew that I was going to need a shower to wake me up. There was no way that I was going to be able to do anything if I didn't have a clear mind.

I looked around at the foreign area around me, realizing that I wasn't in my own element. The flight to California that I had taken the day before instantly replenished my memory, and I started to remember everything that had happened after I had gotten to the dorms. I looked over at my bed. Natalie was still there, asleep. I felt a sick feeling in the bottom of my stomach, and I knew that I had to get out of there.

I gathered all of the things that I needed to get ready and threw them in a large purse. I didn't want to have any reason to come back to the dorms. There was no point. I had made a big mistake, and I wasn't ready to face Natalie yet. How was I going to tell her that everything that happened between us was a mistake? How would she take that? I didn't want to deal with any repercussions resulting from that conversation. I wasn't sure if I could handle it. For that matter, I didn't know if she could handle it. How was I going to tell her that I didn't want to be with her? How were we supposed to live together after that? We were assigned to this dorm for the next few months. This entire situation was about to be awkward if I didn't find a way to deal with it.

I sped into the dorm bathroom, happy that it was empty and hopped into the shower. I had finally remembered why I had set my alarm. I had to be at the internship with Brittney, and I surely didn't want to be late to that. I might as well do something right. This experience had already started off on the wrong foot.

I turned on the shower, letting the warm water wash over my body and soaped myself up. I wanted to wash the memory of the night before away. I wanted everything to make sense again. I wasn't gay. What was I doing? Why did I sleep with Natalie? Maybe, I had a few too many drinks. I wasn't sure, but the thought that I had been with a woman felt very unlike me, and I wanted to scrub every bit of my body and start over.

The shower ended and I got dressed and ready and headed down the hall towards the stairs. I needed to get out of the building before I ran into Natalie. I felt so out of sorts, and the confusion of our night together was replaying in my head. I ran down the stairs and walked out of the dormitory building, towards the bus stop. Maybe if I focused on work, this entire situation would go away. Maybe it wouldn't be as bad as I thought it was. Something had to give. I couldn't go around all day feeling like I was going to throw up.

I closed my eyes. I felt like a person that I didn't know. I wondered if I had just screwed up my life. First, I broke up with Henry. Then, I left for an internship halfway across the country, and now, I had slept with a woman. None of this was like me.

Chapter Thirty-Five

"Well, hello," Brittney beamed as soon as I got into the office. "You're early."

"Sorry about that," I said, forcing a smile.

"Don't be sorry, girl," Brittney replied. "I like a woman that knows what she wants and what she has to do to get it."

I smiled. This woman didn't know anything about me. She had this impression that I was a hard worker and that I was always on point. If only she knew what had happened last night or about my life back home. It was crazy how her image of me was completely different than the one that I had of myself. I felt obligated to live up to the picture of me that she had painted in her head.

"So, how was the ride over here?" Brittney asked.

"Not too bad," I said. "I'm still trying to get used to the city, but I like the fact that there are multiple ways to get around."

"Yeah, it takes a little time to understand which bus goes where, but once you get down the schedule, you can get pretty much anywhere you need to."

I nodded and smiled. I wasn't really in the mood for small talk. I felt like my entire life was collapsing in my lap. I felt like a stranger to myself. I didn't want to talk anymore. I wanted to work. I needed to focus on something that I was good at.

"Well, let's get to work," Brittney said. "I'm going to show you around my shop. I'll show you my website, and maybe, after you see everything, you can tell me what you think and tell me if you see anything that could be improved."

"For sure," I said, happy to get on with the work part of this trip.

Brittney started walking me around, introducing me to everyone else that worked in the shop. She was talking about a mile a minute and I just nodded and smiled to show her that I was listening. However, I wasn't listening. I was thinking about the night that I had with Natalie.

I was thinking about how gentle her fingers were as they caressed my body and how her moan had turned me on.

I had never been into women. I didn't even know how that worked. Was it like having a roommate that you slept with? How did you have a family? Could two women really be in love? These questions plagued my mind as I worked. I felt completely off guard. I didn't feel like I had the foundation that I had always had to rely on. Was there a book that explained what this feeling was? Who could I talk to?

Most people that I knew were straight. I knew a couple of gay people, but I wasn't close to them. Their lifestyle seemed very different from mine. I didn't want to have to change myself. I had grown up knowing that you got married and had children. I had always known what the plan for me was. If I started dating women that would change everything. I might not have the same friends that I had now. I might not have the same career opportunities or the chance to have children. I didn't want to have to give up on my dreams due to my love life. I should have never slept with Natalie. If I had just kept it simple, I could go on like nothing had happened.

I sighed. I was going to have to deal with this situation sooner than later. There was no way that I could go on with so much anxiety and apprehension about my future. I was here to do a job. I wasn't here for romance. I needed to figure myself out.

Chapter Thirty-Six

Work was over and I was back on the bus. I didn't really want to go back to the dorms, so I decided to stop at a coffee shop in Haight Ashbury so I could think about how to deal with Natalie. I ordered a coffee and sat at a table alone, looking at the couples around me. Several of them were gay. It was as if I was surrounded by gay people. Maybe, I was giving off some sort of signal that I was gay. Maybe, everyone knew.

I was freaking out. I took out my phone and dialed my mom. Maybe, she would know what to do. The phone rang and after the fourth ring, I heard it pick up.

"Hi," I said into the receiver, waiting for her to talk so I could gauge what kind of mood she was in.

"Hello," my mom replied. "How are you? How is your internship?"

"Good," I said, not sure how to start the conversation regarding Natalie. "Everything has been going just fine despite one small snafu."

"What snafu?" my mom asked. "Did you get fired? Did they replace you with someone else?"

"No, nothing like that," I replied. "Something occurred in my romantic life."

"Did you meet a new man?" my mom gushed. "I knew you would. There are several successful men in California, and though I do still think you should have stayed with Henry, I had a feeling that you would meet a man on your travels."

"Well...I didn't exactly meet a man," I replied.

"What do you mean?" my mom asked.

"I mean that I met a woman," I said, feeling my stomach bottom out as I said it. My mom was a conservative woman. There was no telling how she would respond to the news.

"A woman?" she inquired. "I thought that you said that there was a development in your romantic life. What does this woman have to do with anything?"

"She is the person that I met," I said. "We hit it off right away. We have a lot of things in common, and then, I ended up waking up next to her."

My mom was silent for a moment. I was sure that she was taking the new information in and trying to figure out how to respond to it.

"So, all of this happened," I continued. "And now I am sitting here, trying to figure out what to do about the situation..."

"Well, you're not gay," my mom replied. "I've known you your entire life and you have never expressed an interest in females. You have always dated men. Maybe, this is one of those college experiences that people are always talking about or a phase. It happens to the best of us. I had a phase in college where I smoked everything I could get my hands on."

"So, you think this is a phase?" I asked. For some reason, her words made me angry. It felt like she wasn't accepting me or my feelings.

"I'm sure this is a phase," my mom replied. "You are in the middle of nowhere. You don't know anyone. People do weird things when they are faced with a situation like that. Find a nice, young man. Go out. Have some fun. I'm sure that after you do that, you will be less confused and more focused on why you went out there in the first place."

"Okay," I said, still not sure that her advice was helpful.

"Trust me," my mom said. "Find a man and go out. You will thank me after you do."

Chapter Thirty-Seven

My mom's words replayed in my head as I left the coffee shop and got back on the bus. Find a man. I couldn't tell if she was being discriminatory towards the idea of me being gay or if she was actually trying to help me. She hadn't flipped out or anything, which I had completely thought she would. She was calm and collected and just told me to find a man. My mom was even understanding. Maybe, she was right. Maybe, my night with Natalie was all because I was in a new place. She said that people did weird things when they were put in new situations, and being halfway across the country from where I lived and the people that I knew was hard to deal with.

On the other hand, my feelings for women hadn't just shown up when I met Natalie. Before I had even considered an attraction to Natalie, I had wondered if I was attracted to Rica, and before Rica, there were several other women that I had a close attachment to back home. I never acted on my feelings. I had always disregarded them. I just couldn't see how a person could be with a person of the same sex and still have the same quality of life that they could have with a person of the opposite sex, but my experiences with partners of the opposite sex hadn't been good either. I was never fully interested in any man that I was dating. They made good friends. I liked talking to them from time to time, but there was never a huge spark.

With Natalie, I had felt more than a spark. I had been excited to explore intimacy with her. I loved the support that she gave me, and so far, I was enjoying the conversations that we had. It felt deeper than anything that I had with a man, and for some reason, it felt right. I actually enjoyed being around Natalie. I liked the way she smelled. I liked the way she laughed, and I liked the fact that she understood me and my point of view. I didn't quite understand the whys in all of it, but I knew that it was a completely different feeling that I had when I was with men, and I wanted to know why that was.

I know what my mom would say. She would tell me that I hadn't met the right man. She would advise me that there were men out there that were great conversationalists and ones that would understand my thoughts and feelings. Ironically, I didn't doubt that there were, but there was just something about being with a woman that made the relationship feel more complete. I couldn't put my finger on it.

The confusion of the situation occupied my mind the entire way back to campus, and then, reality hit. If I started dating women, how would my family and friends react? Would I be faced with more challenges when it came to employment and housing? Would I be sacrificing the opportunity to have a family? The more that these thoughts filled my mind, the more nervous I became about the entire situation. I was young and intelligent and in my prime. I didn't want to ruin any chance that I had at achieving my goals, and if I started dating women, that would put more pressure on my life and everything that I wanted to achieve. I wasn't ready to deal with that, and it seemed smarter to handle the situation in the way that my mom had advised. With that, there was less complication. With that, I still had my dreams and goals and a foreseeable path forward.

Chapter Thirty-Eight

A s I headed back to the dorms, I tried to figure out what I could do to occupy my attention. As much as I wanted to see Natalie, I wasn't ready to talk to her, and knowing that I would have to break her heart by telling her that I couldn't be with her for the sole reason that she was a woman didn't seem like a fun conversation to have. I walked by the gym and it gave me an idea. If I told Natalie that I was going to work out, then I would be able to get out of the dorms and have some time to mull over all of the events that occurred the night before. That would be a good enough excuse to avoid the hard conversation that I was going to have to have with her, and it might even make me feel better.

I smiled at the thought. I needed a way to work out all of the stress in my body. If I didn't get it out then I wouldn't be able to fix the situation that I was in and I might even get wrinkles. I had gone this long without having to endure this kind of stress. Maybe a little workout would help me and maybe in the process of trying to get rid of my anxiety, I would run into a man that fit my criteria. Then, I wouldn't have to deal with coming out or telling my friends and family that I liked women. I could just live. All I needed to do was find that perfect guy.

The dorms came into view and I hurried up the stairs, hoping that I had gotten back before Natalie. I opened the door to our room, noticing that no one was inside and quickly changed out of my work clothes and into a pair of bicycle shorts and a tank top. Just as I got dressed, the door opened and I caught Natalie's eye. Natalie was smiling at me. She layed her phone on the desk in the room and slipped off her shoes.

"How are you doing?" she asked, kissing me gently on the cheek. "You look nice."

"Yeah, I'm going to work out," I said, feeling a little awkward. The spot where her lips had connected with my cheek tingled a bit, and my heart was racing. It was like my body and my mind were doing two different things.

"Do you want company?" Natalie asked. "I brought a set of work-out clothes as well. We could both go, and that would give us a chance to talk about our days."

"No," I said. I felt like I was going to puke. I had to tell her the truth. There was no avoiding it. If I didn't, then she would be walking around, thinking that everything was fine between the two of us, and it didn't seem fair for me to lead her on in that way. "No, I would rather go on my own. It's been a long day, and I feel like a good work-out would help me clear my head. I just want to be alone."

"Oh, okay," Natalie said. "I understand. We all need time to ourselves every once in a while, and with all of the new things that we are going through with this internship, it's probably good for you to take time to process everything."

"Yeah," I said, trying to find the words so I could tell her how I felt. I was at war with myself. Part of me wanted to let her know that the intimacy that we experienced was a one time thing. The other part wanted to leave without saying anything so I didn't hurt her feelings. I knew she would be devastated. It hurt me to know that she would hurt, but I had to tell her the truth.

Chapter Thirty-Nine

I looked at Natalie and sighed. It was now or never. I had to let her know that I didn't plan on continuing our relationships or whatever situation it was that we had going on. "I have to tell you something," I said, knowing that she wasn't going to be happy with what I was going to say. I didn't know what I was going to do if she cried. That would just break my heart, and I knew that I wouldn't already be punished with her sadness when the words came out of my mouth.

"Is everything okay?" Natalie asked. She looked a little nervous, but she just stood there like she had already been expecting the words that were about to come out of my mouth.

"No," I said, shaking my head and looking at the ground. "I just wanted you to know that I can't pursue whatever it is that we have between us any further. I'm not gay. I never have been, and I really don't know what got into me last night."

"Okay," Natalie said. She didn't cry. She didn't look sad or disappointed, but she didn't look happy either. I was having a hard time reading her emotions.

"Okay," I said, looking at her closely. "I'm really sorry. I still want to be friends, and I know that is probably an awkward thing to say, given the circumstances, but I wanted to be completely honest with you."

"Okay," Natalie said once again. She was completely accepting everything that I was telling her. There was no backlash or tears. I didn't understand it. Was she not as into me as I orginally thought that she was? Had she already taken what we had together as a one-night stand? Was that a normal thing in her life?

"Alright then," I said, not knowing what else to say. "I'm going to the gym. I'll be back in a couple of hours."

"See you then," Natalie said, still standing in the same spot when I closed the door.

I was shocked. How could she be so understanding? I barely had to say anything? If it had been me, I would have asked so many questions. I would have wondered if the feelings that we had the night before were real. I would have asked if there was someone else. I would have been devastated, but Natalie had reacted unexpectedly. That reaction had thrown me off. I didn't know where the two of us stood. She seemed to be cordial about the entire situation. She didn't seem like she was holding anything against me, but I wondered if the shock of what I had said would come later. Maybe, she was being coy. Maybe, she had been calm, because she hadn't had time to digest my words.

I didn't know what she was thinking, and though that bothered me, I was happy that there wasn't a blow up. That was the last thing that I needed, to have issues with my roommate while I was trying to concentrate on my future employment. I did my best to clear my head as I got closer to the gym. I no longer had to worry about the situation with Natalie. Now, I needed to figure out my next move, and according to my mom, that was finding a man. Maybe one good screw would rid me of all of the mixed feelings I had been having. It shouldn't be difficult to find a man that was up for that. Most of them basically breathed sex. I walked towards the gym and went through the front doors, feeling the air conditioner blast my skin with an icy chill. It was time to find a man.

Chapter Forty

I put my workout bag in a locker and took my earbuds and phone onto the workout floor. I scanned the room slowly, seeing a treadmill in the right hand corner. It was empty. In fact, most of the machines were. There was only one other person in the gym, a man that was lifting weights, and he didn't look like he was paying attention to me or anything else. I got onto the treadmill and plugged my earbuds into my phone, drowning out most of my thoughts with music. It had been a while since I had worked out. In fact, the last time that I remembered working out was when I lived with Henry. That was when we were good, and we used to work out together. I had fond memories of that time. We would push each other to our goals, and Henry would always do his best to stand near me, especially if I was lifting weights to offer any support that he could.

Henry wasn't all bad. He just wasn't someone that I had fallen in love with. So, it was easier to see all of his flaws than to pay attention to all of the good things that he did. I had always hungered for that spark or to feel some sort of fireworks when the two of us were together, but it never got that far. I had tried to give our relationship a little more time to flourish, wondering if giving it time would open up the doors to more emotions and a deeper connection. However, that never happened. Henry and I did get closer, but it felt more like having a close friend than being with someone that you were so into that you wanted to rip off their clothes and make love to them every time you saw them. The relationship didn't have that it factor. It was bland. I didn't go home, looking forward to having conversations with him. I didn't even want to be around him half of the time. I had thought that I would grow out of having that feeling, but it never happened. So, I left.

When I first left Henry, I blamed it on him. All I could see was all of the things about him that I didn't like, like how he didn't take my career as seriously as I did and how he seemed to act like I was the

81

woman so I needed to tend to the house. Nevertheless, after taking a little time to analyze the relationship that I had with him, it was clear that the main reason that I had left him was because I wasn't happy. He didn't excite me, and that was sad, because if we hadn't never taken the step towards being in a relationship, the two of us might have ended on good terms and as friends.

I sped up the treadmill, hoping to break a sweat and get my heart rate up. Then, I shuffled through my playlist until I came to a more upbeat song. I couldn't spend my entire time in California worrying about relationships. It was obvious that I wasn't good at them, and there was a chance that I would never meet anyone that met the criteria that I had set for a potential partner. I could find a good man, but I never felt a spark. And when I felt a spark, it was with a woman. Maybe, I wasn't meant to be in a relationship. Maybe, I was meant to focus on my career instead. Not every Juliet finds their Romeo, and even if they do, sometimes it ends in tragedy. Focusing on a career seemed so much safer than worrying about all of that chaos.

Chapter Forty-One

I was really getting into my music when I felt a tap on my shoulder. I pulled off my earbuds and looked over, only to see a muscular man on the treadmill next to me. This was clearly not the first time that he had been in a gym. Every arch of his body was rippled with a muscle and he looked solid enough to take most of the men that I had seen on campus. I looked up at his face, noticing his pearly smile and waited for him to say something.

"I wasn't trying to bother you," he said. "I just saw you rocking out to your music, and it made me wonder what you were listening to."

"Oh," I said, holding up my phone. "It's a mix." I started listing off bands and he nodded as if he was truly interested in my choice of music.

"It's crazy how identical our playlists are," he said with a laugh. "For the most part, you just listed most of the songs on my workout track. No wonder you are so focused."

I smiled. It was nice to have something in common with someone who wasn't in the internship program. "And what's your name?" I asked, eyeing his neatly cut beard and soft brown hair.

"Luke," the man said, widening his smile. "And you are..."

"Penny," I said, giving him another once over.

He wasn't bad to look at and he clearly was interested in me. It made me wonder if I should see if he wanted to go out and get that meeting a guy thing that my mom had said to do done. It wasn't like I hadn't gone out with a random man before, and I seemed to be having a nice conversation with this stranger. Maybe, things would progress. Maybe, I just needed to be more open-minded and give someone new a chance.

"How often do you go to the gym?" I asked him, looking at his arms.

"Twice a day," Luke replied, starting his treadmill. "I like to stay in shape. I believe that taking care of your body should be a priority for everyone. I also believe that keeping up with your health affects your mindset throughout the day."

I nodded. What he was saying was making sense, and I truly did agree. I wasn't as passionate as he was, but it was normal for people to have different intensities when talking about different subjects. "So, what do you do after you go to the gym?" I asked, hoping that the conversation would open up a segway so I could ask him out.

"I pick up beautiful women like you," Luke said smiling. "What more is there to life? Work? No. That's not that important. School? I don't think so. But when you see a gorgeous woman standing next to you at the most unexpected place on campus, then there is no doubt that you need to pursue her. You can always get another job or take another class, but there is no replacing an opportunity to meet up with a woman like you."

"I both appreciate the compliment and am very worried about your education and career life."

Luke laughed. "I'm top in my class. I think I'll be fine."

"Top in your class?" I asked. Now, I was impressed. "I didn't know you were so skilled."

"I'm good at other things too," Luke said with a wink. "But you don't have to take my word for it. I'd be willing to show you if you were up for it."

I swallowed hard and looked back at him. Was he suggesting what I thought he was? I guess if I didn't dive in headfirst, I would never find out if sparks could fly with a man the way that they had with Natalie.

Chapter Forty-Two

"Why don't we go now?" I asked, somewhat wondering if he would be willing to leave his workout in order to engage in the activity he was hinting at.

"I'm up for it," Luke said, pushing the button on his treadmill and hopping off. "I'll show you my dorm. It's not far from here."

"Fine," I said, acting like he wasn't getting to me. I really wasn't looking forward to having sex with him, but I felt like I needed to have sex with him in order to know if there was any potential for me to feel intimate with a man. Usually, sex wasn't even fun for me. Sure, once in a while, there would be an orgasm, but more times than not, there wasn't. And even when I did get to that point, it just wasn't satisfying.

The first time that I had felt completely satisfied after having sex was with Natalie. There was no doubt in my mind after we had made love that we were connected mentally and emotionally. The physical part was great too. I had never cum so hard, and I knew that if Natalie was a guy, I wouldn't be standing next to this beefcake that I had met in the gym, trying to replicate the same feelings that I had with her with a man. However, that wasn't the case, and living my life with a woman sounded like both a difficult and unclear path. At least I knew what being with a man was like, and if I could find more of an incentive to date one and stay with one, then it would make my life a lot easier.

"Are you sure you are up for this?" Luke asked, looking over at me. I knew he was trying to be nice, but I could see the giant bulge in his gym shorts, indicating that he was more than ready for a good time.

"I'm ready," I said, smiling at him and running my hand down his bicep. "I just hope you can keep up. I would hate for you to fizzle out as soon as you get it in."

"Don't worry," Luke said. "I have plenty of endurance, and it's been a little while since I have been with a woman, so I'm sure I will show you a good time." He led me into a tall, brick building that was close to the gym and all of the way to the top floor. "And I don't have a roommate, so you don't have to worry about someone walking in on us."

"Good, because I want you to myself for a couple of hours," I said, lying through my teeth. I was nervous. I was oddly excited, but I wasn't exactly turned on by him. I knew I should be, but I wasn't.

Luke led me to his room, closing the door behind him and instantly took me up in his arms, kissing me gently. It was weird kissing a man after kissing Natalie. The stubble felt odd against my face and the fact that he could lift me up the way he could was a little unsettling. I played into it though, kissing him back and allowing him to set me on the bed nearby and pull off my shorts and panties. He quickly took down his shorts, exposing his hard dick and eagerness.

I did my best to cater to him, guiding his hard extremity towards my mouth and letting my lips massage it until I had milked it so hard that it was pouring down my chin. At least that would prevent early ejaculation. Maybe, this time, I would at least cum.

Chapter Forty-Three

"Do you feel better?" I asked, wiping the milky substance from my face and looking up at him.

"Not yet," Luke said, shedding the shorts that were hanging around his ankles, his shoes, and his shirts. "Like I said. It's been a while."

He positioned himself on the bed, pulling me into his lap and removed my shirt and bra, kissing one of my breasts while kneading the other one with his hand. I tried to concentrate on the pleasure of this action, but even though the instinct of sex was there, the feelings for him were not. So, I let myself go to a place where I had felt those feelings. I thought of Natalie. I thought about how she had lightly caressed my nipples with her tongue and about the electricity that ran through my body every time her lips moved across it. At this point, I could feel the warm liquid building up in my center, and as Luke stuck his now stiff dick into me and I rocked back and forth on it, memories of how hard Natalie had made me come played back and forth in my head.

I found that if I focused on her, having sex with Luke wasn't as bad as I thought it would be. Sure, he wasn't really the one that I wanted to be with, and I didn't find him attractive like other women probably would. But I got through it.

Luke had endurance. He made me ride him on the bed before turning me over and getting his final relief while I was in the doggy style position. Then, he positioned me on the desk and fucked me so hard that my head hit the wooden part on the back. He did stop long enough to ask me if I was okay, but then, he got right back to it. Luke was a freak. It was like he didn't have a stop button. I actually got tired before he did, but even when I was tired, he encouraged me to continue pleasuring him, offering me up against the wall and pumping himself inside of me for the third time.

At one point, I started to wonder if he was on steroids or something. He was treating the moment like he had never had sex before, and he wanted to do some kinky stuff. I abided due to the fact that the whole reason that I was there was because I wanted to figure out if I could feel the same way with a man that I had with Natalie, and every time that I had cum with him inside of me, I had been thinking of Natalie and not him. I needed to know that I could focus on him and what he was doing and still get off. I knew that if I was thinking about Natalie the entire time that it was Natalie, not him that was turning me on, and if that was true, then this whole situation had been a mistake.

So, I continued to let him fuck me. I even let him tie my hands behind my back and blindfold me while he did it. I gave him head again, allowing him to choke me a little while he was cumming, and I went for as long as my legs would let me. Finally, after four hours of constant interaction, he was tired. He laid down on the bed, pulling me into his arms and fell asleep. I waited for him to fall asleep before pulling away. I didn't feel anything for Luke, and I didn't really feel like he had fulfilled my physical or emotional needs. Sure, he had fun, but I had been thinking about Natalie the entire time, which could only mean one thing, I was more into her than I was into him.

Chapter Forty-Four

The realization hit me head on as I walked back to my dorm. I was a lesbian. I wasn't bisexual. I had no romantic feelings for men, and though I had been physical with men, it wasn't at all like being physical with a woman. With a woman, I wanted more. With a woman, I felt that emotional connection, and with a woman, I didn't feel the dirty, disgusting feeling that I did now. I wanted to scrub my body until every presence of Luke was gone. I regretted having to sleep with him to have the courage to face the truth, and even the knowledge that I was a lesbian didn't seem as uncomfortable a thing to deal with as having to deal with the memories of the last four hours that I had spent with him.

I made it to my dorm, feeling sick to my stomach. I had really messed things up. I had told Natalie that I wasn't interested in her when I really was. I had slept with a strange guy who had left his mark on every orifice of my body, and the truth regarding my sexual orientation had just hit me head on. I couldn't see a way to dig myself out of the situation that I had put myself in. If I was Natalie, I wouldn't trust me after what I did. I actually felt guilty for doing it. Who sleeps with a woman and then goes right out to sleep with a man just so she can say that she isn't gay? Is that even normal?

I walked into the dorm room, noticing Natalie perched on her bed, reading from her phone. I wasn't sure if she was going to ignore me or talk to me. I didn't even know if we had the same comfort with each other that we had before. Everything could have changed after I told her that I didn't want to be with her. I walked towards my bag, taking out a towel and a clean outfit. I needed to take a shower. I didn't want the memory of Luke to haunt my night.

"Going to shower?" Natalie asked, setting down her phone.

"Yeah," I said, happy that she was still willing to open the door of communication between the two of us. "I just feel gross. I've had an awful day."

"You worked out for a few hours," Natalie replied. "I figured you would come back in a better mood."

"So, did I," I said with a sigh. "But one thing led to another, and I ended up sleeping with this guy. I really screwed up, and I feel so dirty. I'm so sorry for everything that I did to you. I really do have feelings for you, but I was just scared. You see, I can't be gay. It's just not something my friends and family will understand, and now that I know that I am for sure, I don't know what I am going to do. This entire day has been a shit show."

Natalie listened patiently while I rambled. I could tell that she was hurt by some of the things that I was saying, but she never yelled at me or said anything negative to me while I was talking. I didn't understand how someone could have such a close relationship with you and be so patient when you messed up. Natalie wasn't like anyone that I knew.

"Things happen," Natalie replied. "And it wasn't like we were dating. You told me before you left that you couldn't be with me. Maybe, you just need some time to figure out what you want, and if you really are a lesbian, then you might need time to figure out how you want to deal with that, especially if your family isn't on board."

Chapter Forty-Five

I nodded. What she was saying made sense. I needed to figure out myself before trying to get into another relationship, and I needed to figure out how to stand up for myself when it came to my family and friends if I was going to pursue a relationship with a woman. "Thanks for listening to all of this nonsense," I said, looking into Natalie's eyes. "I really didn't mean to hurt you if I did. Everything that we experienced together yesterday was real. My feelings for you are real, and I still want to see where things will go with the two of us."

Natalie looked back at me and nodded. "I want to see where things will go too, but you have to be clear about your intentions first. I don't want to catch more feelings for you only to find out that you didn't give it your all. I want to make sure you are ready to get into a relationship and ready to deal with some of the backlash that comes with dating another female. I would hate to open myself up to you, only to find that you aren't in it one hundred percent."

"So, you do like me?" I asked with a smile. I had been wondering how she felt since I first told her that I didn't want to be in a relationship with her. Her lack of emotion during that first conversation had made me second guess whether what I was feeling between me and her was real, but now, I knew. She felt the same way that I did. She just didn't want to hop into a relationship right away, because she was afraid that I would back out.

"Yeah, I like you," Natalie said. "And I can see my feelings for you growing into something more than that. So, until you are ready to commit yourself to a real relationship, I think that we should just be friends. That gives us more time to get to know each other and more time to see where things can go. It also should give you the time that you need to figure out how you are going to move forth with dating. You might find that I'm not really the person that you want to be with. You might see someone else out there and the two of you might have better chemistry than we did. It's still early. We have only known each other for a couple of days, so it wouldn't be unusual for you to find someone that you like better than me."

I shook my head. "I don't think that will happen," I replied. "I know how I feel, and I have never felt like this about anyone that I have been with or been interested in. However, I do think that you have a point when you say that I need time to think things out. I have to figure out how to break the news to my parents now that I know that I am gay and to my friends. I'm not sure how everyone will react when I tell them, so I want to give them a little time to let the information sink in."

"That's fair," Natalie replied. "I've never been the one to broadcast my sexuality, so this will be new to me too. If we do decide to get into a relationship, I'm going to have to tell my brother and my best friend that I am gay. I haven't really said too much about who I am interested in, so this might be a shock all around."

Chapter Forty-Six

"Are you feeling alright?" Brittney asked, looking at me with compassion.

"I'm fine," I lied. "I'm just a little bit queasy."

Brittney smiled. "Did you go out last night? That would do it to you."

"No," I replied. "I actually haven't drank anything for a while." I wasn't lying either. I hadn't really been into drinking since the night that I ended up in bed with Natalie. Things with Natalie were going good, so I didn't want to chance drinking and having an unexpected situation occur, messing things up. Therefore, I just stayed away from alcohol all together. It wasn't that hard, though I did miss having a glass of wine here and there, and it kept things simple between the two of us.

It had been three weeks since Natalie and I had talked about our relationship. Since then, we had gone out several times, trying to strengthen our friendship before moving on to the next step. We had gone shopping, out for coffee, and even to dinner a few times. It was nice to have someone to explore the new city with, but it was even nicer to have a friendship with a person that was so in-tuned with me.

Natalie and I got each other. We had similar views on life and work and even romance, and we both wanted to succeed and take care of our families. Things were almost perfect between the two of us, but not having that ability to physically express our feelings between each other was difficult. There were several times that I wanted to hold her or kiss her, and I held back, knowing that we had agreed to take things slower than we originally had. Nevertheless, the spark that I had felt with her the night that we had made love was still there, and her body language told me that she felt it too. Now, it was just a matter of getting over that small barrier of telling other people about our sexuality and taking a step forward with commitment in our relationship.

I wasn't sure when that step was going to occur. I had contemplated telling my mom several times, but after thinking about the last phone call that we had, I was sure that she wouldn't get it. The last time that I had talked to her, she had convinced me that all I needed was a man. She had told me that I was going through a stage, and she hadn't really even asked about Natalie. Knowing this, I was worried that she wouldn't acknowledge Natalie or our relationship if the two of us got together, and this made me worry about what would happen if I came back to Chicago after the internship. Would everyone that I knew ignore me? Would I lose all of my acquaintances and friends? I wasn't really sure what I was getting into by coming out to those around me, and it scared me a little.

There were several times that I had thought about just staying in California. It was sunny and warm, and there were a lot of great opportunities working with Brittney. I liked the idea that Natalie had come up with when we first met. She had suggested that Brittney and I merge our companies. This idea seemed like it would give both of us the upper hand as it would give her customers a chance to try my products and my customers a chance to see her methods of advertising and shipping. Eventually, I had plans on talking to Brittney about all of this, but I had been waiting until we knew each other a little better. Things at work had been going smoothly, so I wasn't worried about her looking down on my work ethic, but it just seemed a little early to talk about merging businesses when she was still teaching me the ins and outs as to how hers ran.

Chapter Forty-Seven

"Penny, you really look awful," Brittney said, looking at me again. "If you are sick, feel free to take the rest of the day off so you can relax. I want to make sure that you are in good condition. I don't want you sacrificing your health just so you can learn a thing or two about the business. You already seem to know a lot. It's not like you are going to fall behind."

I looked at her. She seemed to be sincere, and I really wasn't feeling that great. My stomach was churning at this point. It felt like I had a big egg in there floating around my stomach, splashing things around. I didn't get it. I didn't drink. I didn't eat at any new restaurants within the last couple of days, and I didn't feel sick at all when I got up to go to work. It all just hit me out of the blue, and there was no explanation for it.

"I don't feel good," I admitted. "I might take you up on your offer to go home. I don't know what is wrong with me. I felt just fine this morning. I didn't go out. I didn't eat anything unusual, and I don't think I have been around anyone that has been sick."

"I don't know," Brittney said. "But I can't have you sitting here like a sick dog. You aren't going to be able to concentrate on anything. You are going to be thinking about how you feel, and besides that, if you feel as bad as you look, I don't want to catch what you have. I can't afford to take too much time off. I'm a little behind as it is, and I am training you to be able to take over when I can't come in, so I need you in good shape too."

I looked at her. This was the second time that she had said something about promoting me, and she had followed through with paying me while I did the internship. So, if she was serious about me going home, then I was going to take her up on the offer. I didn't want to be useless all week because I didn't take one measly half-day. I wanted to show her that I could handle the responsibility that she was giving me, and if I got that promotion that she kept offering, I would be in a great position to suggest a merge of our companies.

"Well, I'm going to pack up and get going then," I said. "Hopefully, I will feel better tomorrow. It makes me a little nervous to go home when I am supposed to be working though."

"Health before wealth," Brittney replied, winking at me. "I know that you are used to running your own business and having to give up a bunch of your free time, but you have to take care of yourself first. If you don't, then all of the work that you put into your company or mine will be wasted."

"Well said," I replied. "I guess I hadn't thought of it like that."

"You have to," Brittney said. "Losing a couple of hours doesn't even accumulate to losing yourself permanently. Besides, life isn't all work. You have to be able to appreciate the other things out there too."

I nodded. "That would be nice," I said. My stomach started to swirl again and I could feel the blood rush to my face.

"Go home," Brittney said. "And if you still feel bad tomorrow, call me. I have information on a couple of local doctors that would probably be willing to see you on short notice."

Chapter Forty-Eight

The ride back to campus had been a rocky one, and the walk back to the dorms wasn't much better. I felt so sick that just walking up the stairs and down the hall to my room was a challenge. After unlocking the door to my room, I got to my bed and plopped down. I didn't know if I was going to throw up or not. It felt like there was a gallon of water swimming up and down my throat, and I just wanted it all to stop. I curled up into a tight ball, hoping that changing positions would help calm things down and I closed my eyes.

I really had no clue what could have caused me to be this sick. It was like it came out of nowhere. I thought about all of the food that I had eaten over the last seventy-two hours. Nothing stood out as something that would make me this ill. Then, I tried to remember all of the people that I had come in contact with for more than a couple of minutes at a time. I didn't spend much time with anyone but Natalie. We had talked to a couple of people that we had met in the city, but there was no prominent memory of me even being around a person that was this sick.

I sighed. This sucked. I didn't want to feel this way. I wanted to be able to move around and get done with work and be able to do stuff afterwards. Natalie and I had planned to check out one of the parks in the area when we both got done with our internships. We were going to go on a nice walk and get some coffee. It was supposed to be a peaceful day, but now that I was feeling like my intestines were creeping into my throat, I wasn't sure that I was even going to be able to go. Irritated, I put my face into my pillow and tried not to scream. I was so mad about my day being ruined that it wasn't funny, and I didn't know what to do to make myself feel better.

• • • •

I HEARD THE DOOR CREAK open and I instantly opened my eyes. I must have fallen asleep. I wiped the drool from my cheek and looked up to see where the source of the noise was coming from, only to see Natalie at the door.

"You're home early," she said, closing the door to the dorm room and locking it.

I watched as she put away her work stuff and changed into a more comfortable set of clothes, plopping on her bed after she did. "I'm sick," I said, but at this point, my stomach didn't hurt at all. I wasn't sure if the nap had made me feel better or if whatever illness I had just rolled over.

"With what?" Natalie asked, looking at me closely. "You seemed just fine last night. Was it something we ate?"

I shook my head. "I don't think so," I said. "I thought about that too, but we didn't eat anything out of the ordinary."

"Well, is it your stomach or something else?" Natalie asked. "I had seen you grabbing your stomach, so I just assumed that was what you were talking about."

"Yeah, it's my stomach," I confirmed. "One minute, I was fine. Then, I wasn't. Then, I was again."

"That's weird," Natalie said, looking at me closely. "When did this all start?"

"This afternoon," I said. "I woke up just fine. Then, after I was at work for a couple of hours, everything went downhill."

"That's not good," Natalie said, shaking her head. "Hopefully, no one got you sick."

Chapter Forty-Nine

"My sentiments exactly," I said. "Except it would be weird if it did. I don't remember being around anyone that was sick. I don't remember eating anything that could make me sick, and the feeling didn't even occur until a few hours after I had gotten to work. It's so weird. One minute, I will feel like I have an egg bouncing around in my stomach. The next minute, I feel like there is a gallon of water running up and down my throat. I have never felt this way before, and I am not exactly sure what to do to fix it."

Natalie thought about this for a moment. Then, she ticked her figure up in the air as if she had an idea. "Did you say egg?"

"Yeah," I said, not sure what relevance that was to the topic at hand. "Why?"

"What if you aren't sick?" Natalie asked. "What if this is something else?"

"Like what?" I asked. I didn't know what was going through her head. It wasn't like I was making the entire thing up. I genuinely felt bad while I was at work

"Like what if your nausea is a symptom of something else?" Natalie asked. "You did just sleep with that guy a few weeks back. Have you taken a pregnancy test?"

"A pregnancy test?" I asked. I was outraged. "How could I have gotten pregnant? I have slept with men before. I never got pregnant then."

"Are you on birth control?" Natalie asked. "Because I'm not trying to be all up in your business, but I haven't seen you take any since you have been here."

"No," I replied. "I stopped taking that a while ago before I even broke up with Henry."

"Did you use a condom?" Natalie asked.

Now, she was really getting on my nerves, not just because she was asking so many questions but because some of the questions that she was asking were legitimate. I hadn't used a condom when I was with Luke. I hadn't even thought about it. The only thing that I had been thinking about in that moment was that I had to prove to myself that I wasn't gay. I was more focused on following my mom's advice and finding a man than in using protection during sex, and now that I had a little time to think about the entire situation, I realized how stupid the whole thing really was. Not only did I not prove that I was straight but now, I might have gotten myself pregnant.

This was not the time to get pregnant. I had just gotten to a new city. I had a potential promotion in my future, and I was trying to get to know Natalie and possibly take things to the next step. If I had a baby while all of this was going on, there was a chance that I was going to have to give up something else that I had been working on, and that was devastating.

"So, did you?" Natalie asked, looking at me closely. "I think that I know the answer due to the look on your face, but I just want to confirm."

"No, I didn't," I said, dropping my head. I needed to get tested and fast. If my life was going to change this quickly, there were a lot of things that I needed to figure out. Like, where would I have the better? Would I tell Luke? Didn't he deserve to know? If I did tell him, would he try to be a part of my life or would he just focus on the relationship with his child? And what about the internship and Natalie?

Chapter Fifty

"You look like you are going to breakdown," Natalie said, coming over so she could sit next to me. "It will all be okay. Things happen, and whatever happens can be handled."

I looked at her. "You know that I will keep the baby if I am pregnant, don't you?" I asked, trying to see how she responded emotionally to my words.

"I would hope so," Natalie replied. "As a person that never really got to have a relationship with my biological parents, I would hope that you would do everything that you could to make that little one's life the best that it could be."

"But what about us?" I asked, nervous to know what she would say.

"What about it?" Natalie asked with a shrug. "Shit happens. Then, you move on. Just because you might be pregnant, doesn't mean we can't still work on us. You will have to figure things out with the father though. I think he deserves to know if that happens to be the case."

"Yeah," I said. "I was thinking about that. I don't want to be with him though, so I hope he doesn't expect us to get into a relationship and get married or anything like that. I'm not in love with him. It was just a one-night stand."

"You will just have to make that clear to him," Natalie said. "Set boundaries, and if he wants to be a part of the child's life, then let him."

"Yeah," I said. My mind was swirling at this point. There were so many things to consider if it turned out that I was pregnant. I would have to tell Brittney. I would have to find a doctor, and I would have to tell my parents. That would be the hard part, telling them that I was pregnant and that I didn't want anything to do with the father. They would probably want to meet him and have me stay with him. I wasn't up for that.

I had been so worried about coming out to my parents for so long that I hadn't thought that there might be something worse that I had to tell them. Now, that I had to tell them that I was pregnant due to a one-night stand and that my entire future might change in the blink of an eye, telling them that I was into women didn't really seem like that big of a deal. I should have just stood my ground with my mom when I first had that talk with her. If I had, I might not have ended up in this position. Instead, I would have been off with Natalie, having a good time, enjoying life and not having to worry about any added responsibility.

"We need to get that test," I said. "Maybe, we should buy three. I would hate to get a negative only to find out that the next one is positive."

"Well, we need to go into the city then," Natalie replied. "I wanted to pick up a couple of snacks anyhow. Maybe, we could go to the gas station that is by that chocolate shop. I've been hankering for some good chocolate."

"That works for me," I said, completely stressed at this point. Something told me that everything would work out, but not knowing how it would work out was what unnerved me. "I need to figure this thing out. If I am pregnant, I am going to have to see a doctor."

Natalie nodded. "That's for sure, and you are also going to have to figure out what you can and can't do. Obviously, you can't drink alcohol when you are expecting, but I heard that you couldn't eat deli meat either."

"Really?" I asked, wondering where she had heard such nonsense. I couldn't imagine that my diet would have to change that drastically. I basically ate subs and salads and I drank tea, not soda.

Chapter Fifty-One

"You made it out like you were coming down here to get pregnancy tests, but really it was all about the chocolate, wasn't it?" I asked Natalie as I watched her load bag upon bag with various chocolate candies and desserts.

"I can't help it," Natalie said with a smile. "San Francisco has some of the best sweet shops that I have seen. I plan on taking advantage of all that they offer, especially if it's something that will arouse my tastebuds."

"So, that's what arouses you," I commented, giving her a look.

"One of the things," Natalie said with a smile. "Do you want me to get you some?" she asked, turning her attention back to her haul.

"No," I replied. "Eating chocolate sounds like more of a chore than a treat. It kind of makes me queasy thinking about it."

"Oh, that's too bad," Natalie said with a compassionate look. "It's probably your hormones. They heighten when you are pregnant, and that could make your stomach roll. I'll bet you start eating food that you never thought you would touch. A lot of women like pickles, at least that's what I've heard."

"We don't even know if I am pregnant," I replied, lifting up the bag with the tests in it. "We still need to figure that out."

"I told you to go into the gas station bathroom and use the test," Natalie said. "Then, we would know right away."

"No," I said, shaking my head. "Do you know how many germs are in those bathrooms? What if I accidentally get someone else's sample on the stick? I don't want a false positive. I want to be for sure."

Natalie laughed. "I don't think you would get someone else's sample on there, unless you stuck the stick straight on the toilet, but if you don't want to take the test until we get back, that's fine."

"Well, I'm glad that I got your approval," I said sarcastically.

"The pleasure is all mine," Natalie said with a wide smile.

I shook my head. She sure could be sarcastic at times, but this wasn't exactly the right time for that kind of behavior. I really was worried about tainting my sample. I wanted to be as careful as I could when taking the pregnancy test. I didn't want to worry about a whole bunch of external factors messing up my test.

"Come on," Natalie said, pulling me towards the front counter. "Let me get checked out and then, we can go back home and check these tests out."

"Okay," I said, feeling a little relief. The question as to whether or not I was pregnant was killing me. I wanted to know what I was dealing with, and if I was pregnant, I wanted to come up with some kind of plan as to how I was going to handle that.

Natalie paid for her candy, and we walked back to the bus stop to wait for the next ride. Several other people gathered at the stop while we were there, one in particular, getting my attention. I looked over at the blonde to my right and she looked back at me with a smile. It was Brittney. I hadn't expected to run into her, and I didn't know how to explain why I was off campus with Natalie and a bag full of candy. I did my best to prepare myself as she walked closer to me, thinking about how I was going to explain the situation, especially when just hours ago, I had to leave my internship early.

Chapter Fifty-Two

"Fancy meeting you here," Brittney said, looking me over. "You look a lot better than you did earlier."

"I don't know about that," Natalie said, lifting the bag of pregnancy tests that was in my hand.

"What's that?" Brittney asked, eyeing the bag.

I could feel my face turning red. I hadn't quite prepared myself to explain the pregnancy tests. I gave Natalie a look and then looked over at Brittney. She looked skeptical, so I waved her closer and let her look in my bag.

Brittney's eyes grew wide and she looked me over once again, this time concentrating on my stomach. "I didn't know," she replied. "But that explains the nausea."

"I don't know for sure yet," I said. "I still have to take the tests, hence the reason they are in the bag."

"Did you do something that..." Brittney started.

I already knew what she was going to ask. "Yes, I did, but it was a mistake."

"So, you aren't dating the person?" she questioned. "Does he even know?"

"No," I said, shaking my head. "And hopefully, it will come back negative, so I never have to talk to him again."

Brittney raised her eyebrows. "Was it consensual?"

"Yes," I nodded.

"Sorry," Brittney replied. "I don't mean to be so invasive. It's just you looked so disappointed when I mentioned the guy. I wanted to make sure that you didn't have anything happen to you."

"No, I didn't," I said. "It was a mistake, but it was consensual. I was trying to test things out."

"For what?" Brittney asked.

"To see if I was attracted to him," I replied.

"You know, there are other ways to see if you are attracted to someone," Brittney said with a laugh.

"That's not what I mean," I said seriously. Brittney already knew more about me than I was comfortable with. I wasn't used to mixing business with pleasure, and though I wanted to put a halt to the conversation, I felt obligated to explain myself.

"What do you mean then?" Brittney asked, looking me in the eyes.

I waved her closer and got on my tippy toes so I could whisper in her ear. "I was trying to see if I was still straight, so I slept with him."

I pulled back and looked at her face. Brittney looked very confused. "Did you hear what I said?" I asked, wondering if she was judging me.

"Yeah, I did," Brittney said, still wearing the same look. "Girl, I think we need to go out for coffee. You are going to have to tell me more about this whole situation when we have more time to talk."

I nodded. It was a little hard to have the conversation with everyone on the street walking by us, and I could tell that the details that I had given her about what was going on didn't make sense to her. "Fine, we can schedule a time to have coffee," I said. "I'll talk to you more about making plans tomorrow when I see you at work."

"Sounds good," Brittney said, turning around.

"I thought you were waiting for the bus," I called.

Brittney turned around. "No," she said. "I drove here. I just wanted to see why you were in the city."

I waited for her to walk down the sidewalk and away from the bus stop before turning to Natalie. "I think that I almost got fired," I said, my nerves reeling.

"No," Natalie said, shaking her head. "She seemed genuinely worried about you. She probably just wanted to make sure that you were alright."

"I don't know about that," I said, looking once again at the spot where Brittney had stood only moments ago. "What is the chance that she was in the same area we were at the same time? Finding someone here is like finding a needle in a haystack."

Natalie rolled her eyes. "You are reading too much into it. We need to get you home and get you tested. Let's focus on that. If that test is positive, then we will have bigger fish to fry than running into Brittney."

Chapter Fifty-Three

I stood in the bathroom stall, staring at the test. This was the third time that I had taken a test, and I had the same results. I couldn't believe it. It was one thing, trying to think of what you would do if you were pregnant. It was another thing, finding out that you were. I was anxious. I was scared, but surprisingly, I was a little happy. I was going to have the chance to be a mother. I had never really thought too in depth about having kids. My parents made it seem like my birth had hindered some of their plans, so being a mother wasn't at the top of my priority list, especially since I was working on my career.

However, knowing that I was a mother and that there was a little person growing inside of my stomach changed things. Though I was still concerned with my career, I was now worried about being a good parent. I wanted to get things in order so my little one had everything that he or she needed when she arrived. It was almost as if everything was a bit clearer. All of the things that I was worried about before didn't really matter. Now, the most important person in my life was my kid, and I needed to do what I needed to do to take care of him or her.

I still had a couple of months at the internship program, but I needed to figure out what I was going to do after that. Unlike some of the other women, I didn't come straight out of high school. I was a little older, and I had already owned my own house and had a life that was seemingly established. So, the thought that I would have to figure out where I wanted to settle down wasn't as scary as it probably would have been if I was a bit younger.

I didn't really want to go back to Chicago. That would just be awkward. I didn't want the people that I knew to be in all of my business and judge me for the new turn that my life had taken, but I knew that if I stayed in California, I would have to find a place to stay permanently. I would have to rebuild my life, make new friends, and find out how I fit in. Though that sounded like a lot of work, it sounded like the most promising decision. At least, I would have a job out here if everything else failed, and I had started to familiarize myself with the city, so it might not be as big of an adjustment as it seemed.

Then, there was Natalie. The more time that I spent with her, the more my feelings had grown for her. As dumb as it sounded, I was sure that I was falling in love, but I knew that after the internship ended, she would probably go back to Texas. She wanted to live in the same city as her brother, and she was very close to her best friend, Sharise. I knew that I couldn't ask her to drop everything just to move here. It wouldn't be fair. She had her own life to attend to, and even though I didn't want her to give that up, I was sad that our future might not work out.

I looked back down at the stick in my hand and out the slit of the bathroom stall door. "Natalie, it's positive," I said. "I'm pretty sure that this is my confirmation."

Chapter Fifty-Four

"Come out here," Natalie said.

I flushed the toilet and walked out of the stall. She instantly came around my shoulder and peeked at the test. "See, there are two lines," I said. "It's not even that faint."

"Oh, wow," Natalie said. "Well, throw it away and wash your hands. I guess we have something to celebrate."

"Yeah," I said. I was happy, but I was also worried about everything else. I needed to figure out my living situation, and I needed to talk to Natalie about my decisions. I didn't want her to put her emotions into a possible future relationship when there might not be a chance for the two of us to be together.

"You also need to tell Luke," Natalie said. "Maybe, we should do that before we celebrate. That might be difficult, and I would rather end the night on a good note."

I thought about how it would be to tell Luke that I was pregnant. I didn't really know too much about the guy. He seemed like he was used to having one-night stands, and I was pretty sure that he wasn't going to be happy when he found out that I was pregnant. "Will you come with me?" I asked, looking over at Natalie. "I'm really not sure how he will take it, and if he is the aggressive type, I would rather have backup."

"Yeah, that's fine," Natalie said. "Do you have a way to get ahold of him?"

"No," I said. "But I'm pretty sure that we will find him at the gym. This is about the same time that I saw him at the gym last time that I was there, and if he is committed to working out, he probably keeps about the same schedule."

"Let's try it," Natalie said. "If we go now, we can get it over with. What are you going to do if he doesn't want to be any part of it?"

"Honestly, I would rather that he wasn't," I admitted. "It's easier for me to do things on my own than to work with someone else. I would rather not be hooked to a man that I slept with once for the rest of my life."

"You slept with him multiple times," Natalie replied, looking down at the ground. "But I get it."

We were both silent for a minute. I could tell that the fact that I had slept with Luke had hurt her deeply, and I knew that wasn't something that I could ever take back. However, I hoped she would forgive me at some point, because I had made it clear that the only reason I had been with him in the first time was to explore my identity, and at this point, I knew that I was attracted to her, not him.

We made it down the hall and out of the dorms, and I started to think of how to word things with Luke. This would probably be a huge surprise to him, and if he did decide to be a part of the baby's life, we would have to figure out how he could be part of all of the milestones without the two of us having to compromise our individual lives. I was strongly hoping that he wasn't the type that felt obligated to propose just because there was a baby, and I was nervous that he would try to start a relationship with me. I really didn't want anything to do with him. It wasn't that he was a bad guy. He just wasn't for me.

Chapter Fifty-Five

We walked into the gym, and I instantly saw Luke. He was on an exercise bike, talking to the female next to him. That must be his thing, talking to women that he met at the gym. I shook my head, even more irritated that I had slept with him and started to walk towards him. I was hoping that this conversation would be short and sweet, and I knew that if I interrupted the little situation that he had going on with the woman next to him, he probably would hope for the same thing.

"Hi, Luke," I said, catching his attention and flashing him a big smile. "Can I talk to you for a minute?"

Natalie was at my side. She remained silent, but I could tell that she was giving Luke a once over, probably trying to figure out what it was that I saw in him. I tried to hide my smile. It was kind of cute that she was sizing him up. If only she saw what I saw in her then she wouldn't be so worried.

"Hey..." Luke said, turning around and looking at me. He stopped his exercise bike and walked over me, and as he did, I could see the woman next to him give me a warning look.

I smiled at the other woman. Obviously, she saw me as competition, but I was soon going to make it clear that I wasn't even in the running.

"How are you doing?" Luke asked, giving me a sweaty hug even though none of my body language signaled that I wanted one.

"Good," I said. "We need to talk. Do you want to talk here or do you want to go out into the hall?"

"Here's fine," Luke said. "There's nothing that we are going to say that Cheryl can't hear," he commented, signaling over to the woman that he had been working out next to.

"Shari," the woman corrected him, but Luke didn't even acknowledge her.

"So, what's up?" he asked, taking a towel and dabbing his forehead. "Did you want to go out again? I've missed you..."

"Penny," I said. This guy wasn't great with names.

"Right, Penny," Luke said with a smile. "I knew that."

"And no, I don't want to go out again," I replied. "I am actually seeing someone else."

"Who?" Luke asked, looking around the gym as if he was going to find another man that looked like he was with me.

"Me," Natalie said, looking Luke in the eyes. She didn't waver.

Luke blushed and then smiled at Natalie. "Well, we could make it a party," he suggested, looking back at Natalie and then at me.

"I don't roll that way," Natalie said. "We actually came here to tell you something else."

"What?" Luke asked, still dabbing himself with a towel.

"I'm pregnant," I replied.

I don't know what I expected. Maybe, I thought that he was going to be shocked. Maybe, I thought he would get angry, but Luke didn't do anything different than what he was doing. It was as if he hadn't heard me.

"Did you hear what I said?" I asked, wondering if by chance I hadn't said it loud enough.

"Yeah," Luke said, putting his hand up as to stop me from repeating myself. "I heard. Are you sure it's mine?"

"Yes," I said. "I haven't been with anyone else...any other man anyhow."

"Okay," Luke said, putting his hand in his shorts' pocket and retrieving a wallet. "How much do you want?"

I looked at him closely. Was he serious? He thought that I came here for money. Didn't he want to know more about the baby? Didn't he want to be a part of the child's life? I mean, as much as I didn't want to be connected to him for the rest of my life, I couldn't imagine just giving up a baby or paying someone off. What was wrong with him?

Chapter Fifty-Six

"I don't want your money," I replied, taking Luke off guard. "I wanted to see what you wanted to do about this situation. Do you want to be involved? Do you want partial custody? Do you want to be there when your child is born?"

Luke shook his head. "Not necessary," he said. "You do whatever you want with the kid. I've got too much on my plate to be worrying about an extra responsibility."

I was stunned. I mean, I had heard of guys that weren't very involved in their child's life, but this was just too much. This man was okay with going around and making babies and just paying off the mothers so he didn't have to do anything. How could anyone be so heartless? I had spent my entire life accidentally breaking men's hearts due to the fact that I wasn't in love with him, but this was a different kind of heartbreak. This one hurt deep. I was sad for my child.

"Well, I will send you the custody papers, and I would like for you to sign full custody over to me then," I said, trying not to let my feelings show. "I don't want to be playing cat and mouse for the rest of my life."

"Will do," Luke said with a fake salute.

I shook my head. "Do you have other kids?"

Luke looked back at me and smiled. "Yeah, I have a few," he said.

"How many?" I asked, wondering if this was a situation that he had been in before.

Luke started counting on his fingers, and when he got to the second hand, my stomach started to roll. "Five...no six...Wait, there is a set of twins, so seven I guess."

"Wow," I said. "And you aren't a part of any of their lives?"

"They all have moms," Luke replied. "And I pay for them. What more do they need? A lot of kids grow up without having a dad."

I sighed. I couldn't take this guy anymore. "Bye, Luke," I said, walking away.

Natalie followed. "That guy is a major piece of work," she said as soon as we made it out of the gym door.

"You're telling me," I said. "I can't believe that I slept with him." I rubbed my stomach. I was all emotional.

"Are you sure that you are over him?" Natalie asked. "You sure are crying a lot."

"I never was into him," I replied. "I was into you, and I still am. I am just upset that he is willing to sacrifice his relationship with our child just so he can do whatever it is that he wants to do. It's not fair to the child. There are so many people that don't even get to meet their parents, and I don't get how he doesn't want to give this child a fair chance."

"He's a player," Natalie replied, rubbing my back. "Let's get back to the dorms. We are supposed to be celebrating, not worrying about jerks like him. Maybe, we can change and go out to eat. That will be a good celebration for both you and baby."

"That sounds nice," I said, wiping my tears. I was still sniffling, but now, my stomach was growling too. Maybe, a good meal would turn this day around.

"It does sound nice," Natalie said. "And this would be our first meal as a couple."

"A couple?" I asked. "Are you sure you want to make it official? Look at everything that has happened."

"Do you want to be with me?" Natalie asked.

"Yes," I said. "But I thought that we needed to give time. We were going to come out to our families, and we were going to see where things went."

"Well, I guess I have news too," Natalie replied.

I looked at her closely. "What's that?"

"I came out to my brother and Sharise earlier today," she said. "Ironically, they weren't even surprised, and apparently, the two of them hooked up. They will be flying into town next week, so you can meet them."

"Wow," I said. I was extremely excited to finally confirm our plans to move forward as a couple, but there were still a couple of loose ends. "What about after the internship? What about the baby?"

"Shh," Natalie said, pressing her finger to her lips. "We will figure all of that out later."

Chapter Fifty-Seven

We were getting ready for dinner. Natalie had gone off to the showers, and I was in the room, going through my clothes to see if there was something that fit me comfortably, when my phone rang. It was my mom. I sighed. I needed to talk to her anyhow, and since Natalie had already come out to her brother and best friend, I felt obligated to do the same thing. I answered the phone, bracing myself for the conversation I was about to have.

"Hello," my mother said into the receiver. "Penny, is everything alright?"

"Yes," I said. "Everything is finally alright."

"What do you mean by that?" my mother asked, an obvious suspicion in her tone.

"I mean, I'm gay, mom," I said. "I tried what you said, and it didn't work. I'm falling in love with a woman that I met here. Her name is Natalie, and she is the kindest, most compassionate individual that I have ever met. I'm going to see where things go with her."

"But..." my mom said.

"There's more," I said, interrupting her. "I'm pregnant, and I'm moving to California. It's about time that I see what it's like to live the life that I want, one where no one tells me what is proper and what isn't proper. I want to be myself. I'm tired of everyone else's expectations preventing me from living the life that I want to live."

"Penny?" my mom replied. "Pregnant?"

"Yes," I said calmly. "I'm going to schedule a doctor's appointment later this week to see how far along I am. I will let you know. You are more than welcome to come down here and see the birth of your first grandchild, and while you are down here, you can meet Natalie."

"This is so much," my mom replied. She sounded frantic. "Are you sure this is what you want to do? Do you want me to call Henry and tell him about the baby?"

"No," I said. "The baby isn't his, and the father of the baby doesn't want anything to do with the situation."

"I'm extremely concerned for your wellbeing," my mother said. "Maybe, you should just come home. It sounds like being in California has been more of a burden than anything else."

"Being in California has shown me that I can survive on my own feet," I countered. "I know now that I can be who I want to be without having to worry that there won't be people there for me. I can live the life that I want to live and be happy, and I feel like I am doing a better job at making a life for myself out here than I ever did in Chicago. I'm staying here."

My mom was silent for a moment. It was clear that she was taking everything in, and it was a lot to take in so I didn't want to pressure her to digest everything in one sitting. "Oh, wow," she finally said. "I'm going to have to tell your father. I'm not sure what he is going to think about all of this."

"Tell him," I said. "And let me know if you want to come down here and visit. I'll send you pictures of the ultrasounds and keep you up to date on what is going on with the baby. Take some time to think about everything. It's a lot. I get it, but it is my life, and this is the choice that I am making."

"Well, I love you," my mom said. She sounded like she was on the brink of tears.

"I love you, too," I said, trying not to cry myself. I felt for my mom. She grew up in a conservative environment, and everything that was happening in my life was probably a big shock to her. "I'll talk to you later," I said, hanging up the phone. Then, I bawled, because the intensity of the situation just overtook me.

Chapter Fifty-Eight

"You look nice," Penny said as we walked out of the dorms and towards the bus stop.

"Thank you," I said, looking down at my attire. It really didn't look as good as I had thought it would. My shirt was too tight, and my pants felt like a rubberband around my waist. I hadn't grown a lot, but I had grown enough that my regular clothes were uncomfortable.

I looked up at the sky. The moon was dancing above our heads. It reminded me of the first night that we had gotten together. "It's a beautiful night," I said, looking over at Natalie.

"That it is," Natalie replied, putting her hand in mine. "Come here for a minute. I have something to show you."

I followed her to the side of the dorms, noticing a small twinkle in the distance. "What's that?" I asked, walking closer.

"Let's go look," Natalie replied, leading me towards the beautiful lights.

As we walked closer I noticed a small table with a white table cloth. There were small lights in the grass, illuminating the table with a soft glow and a battery-operated candle in the center of the table. A plate was on either side of the candle as was a set of silverware, and there were two wine glasses at each setting.

"Did you do this?" I asked, looking over at Natalie. "This is..." I couldn't find the words to express my emotions.

"I'm glad you like it," Natalie said, letting go of my hand, so she could pull a chair out for me. "I had to make a couple of phone calls, but surprisingly Christina was willing to help with everything. The food will be delivered soon from her restaurant. I tried to work with your diet, so you should be able to eat everything they bring."

"When did you do all of this?" I asked, looking around. "I've been with you pretty much since I got off of work."

"Remember that shower?" Natalie asked with a laugh. "I showered earlier this morning, so I took the time that I was supposed to be in the shower to contact Christina. We're not close, but Brittney was there with her and since she liked my idea, Christina agreed to help. Then, I talked to a couple of people in the dorms to see if they had an extra table and a couple of chairs and a tablecloth. You would be surprised what people around here have. I set everything up while you were getting ready, and voila!"

I smiled at Natalie. "This is probably the most romantic thing that anyone has done for me," I said. "And the fact that you did it where we had our first kiss just makes everything ten times better."

Natalie smiled and then looked down at the table before looking back up at me. "I'm falling for you, Penny," she said quietly. "I don't understand how this is happening so soon, but I'm in it for the long haul. I wanted to show you how much I care about you. I know that I can't expect it, but I do hope that you feel the same way."

I curled my fingers over her palms, feeling the warmth of her skin. "I feel the same way," I said. "I even called my mom and told her. I'm ready to start fresh. I want to see where this goes."

Natalie looked into my eyes, and I could feel the chemistry between us. I leaned forward, connecting my lips with hers. Just like before, everything around us fell away. It was just us and the temperate night and the glowing moonlight. I could feel the passion between us as we caressed each other's lips and I knew that I had made the right choice. I was in love with Natalie.

Chapter Fifty-Nine

Epilogue

"**D**o you need any juice?" my mom asked, pacing around the living room as if she didn't know what to do.

"No, I'm fine," I said, cuddling Eric in my arms. "He's finally asleep and at peace. I don't want to wake him by reaching over for my glass."

"Yeah, he's been up all night," Natalie said, popping her head out of the kitchen. "I came home last night from the restaurant, and I could hear him crying as soon as I was standing in front of the door. Penny looked like she was about to drop out, so I stayed up with him for a couple of hours until we could get him back to sleep."

"I don't know what your brother and Sharise are going to do when they come down here," I commented. "Eric isn't much of a sleeper. As soon as the moon comes out, he is ready to party."

"Must be genetics," Natalie said, giving me a wink.

"Well, I'm glad that the two of you found a place," my mom said, sitting on the couch. "I was worried, but now that both of you have found jobs and have a place to live, I suppose I can sleep much easier."

"Yeah, I was pretty glad that Brittney decided to keep me on," I said. "She didn't even care that I wanted to take some time off to get used to having Eric around. She was almost throwing me out the door."

"It must be his cute smile," Natalie said, coming over to look at the sleeping baby in my arms. "He even melted Christina's heart, and for the longest time, I didn't think that was possible."

"Eric has a way of doing that," I said, smiling at my baby. "I'm just glad that Christina and you are getting along better. I was so happy when she hired you full-time."

"Me too," Natalie replied. "If it wasn't for our new jobs, we wouldn't have the money to afford this house or the thousand items that we needed to buy to take care of him. I'm really happy that it all worked out."

"So, when is your brother coming?" I asked, looking over at the clock. "Didn't you say that his plane came in today?"

"Yeah, in about an hour," Natalie said. She turned to my mom and smiled. "Mrs. Brookington, are you sure that you are okay with watching Eric while we pick up Trent and Sharise?"

"I didn't fly all of the way out here for nothing," my mom replied with a smile. "I want to spend some time with the little booger. I'd be holding him now had it not taken so long to get him down for a nap."

"Well, we are going to have to leave soon," I said. "Do you want to see if you can switch me over? I think if we are gentle, he will stay asleep."

"Let's do it," my mom said.

She sat down on the couch next to me and we slowly slipped Eric into her arms. I looked at him and smiled. He was still making little snoring noises. "Well, I guess that's it," I said, somewhat reluctant to leave my baby for the first time, even if it was with my mom. "We will be back in a little bit. We need to leave soon or we won't be able to beat traffic."

"Go along," my mom said, waving her hand. "He will be fine."

I nodded and turned towards Natalie. "Are you ready?"

"I am," she said, slipping her arm around my waist. "Don't worry so much. Your mom has this handled. She's done this before."

"Listen to your fiance," my mom called, obviously overhearing our conversation.

"I will," I said, looking back and smiling at my mom. It had taken some time, but she had finally come around. She loved Natalie. She loved Eric, and now, Natalie and I were about to integrate her family into our little one. Things were right were they needed to be, and I was finally happy.

Don't miss out!

Visit the website below and you can sign up to receive emails whenever Nicole Higginbotham-Hogue publishes a new book. There's no charge and no obligation.

https://books2read.com/r/B-A-WPSJ-EPDOC

BOOKS 2 READ

Connecting independent readers to independent writers.

Did you love *The Heartbreaker*? Then you should read *Beyond the Lights*[1] by Nicole Higginbotham-Hogue!

Sawyer Johnson has spent her entire life in the same small town with the same people, and she has always imagined a life beyond the bright lights of the town. Autumn Thompson, her best friend is completely satisfied with their simple lifestyle and can't imagine anything coming in between them. However, when Sawyer decides to go on a trip out of town in order to meet her celebrity crush, Autumn insists on going with her. Will Sawyer find happiness in a lifestyle framed around fame and fortune, or will Autumn finally convince her that the life that they had together was worth more than she thought?

Read more at www.higginbothampublications.com.

---

1. https://books2read.com/u/49M6aM

2. https://books2read.com/u/49M6aM

Also by Nicole Higginbotham-Hogue

Jems and Jamz
Don't Tell Me Twice
A Second Chance
To the Beat of Their Own Drum
Finding a Voice
A Fan to Remember
Aspiring Affection
A Stepping Stone
The Jems and Jamz Series: Books 1-2
The Jems and Jamz Series: Books 3-4
The Jems and Jamz Series: Books 5-7
The Jems and Jamz Series Boxset

Le coffret de la série Jems et Jamz
Le coffret de la série Jems et Jamz
Trouver une voix
Affection aspirante
Un tremplin

Simmons Series

A Brief Debacle
A Bit of a Pickle
The Catnip Conundrum
The Simmons Series: Books 1-2

The Avery Detective Series
Sentiment to the Heart
Sentiment to the Heart
Heart's Content
Complicated Heart
The Avery Detective Series: Books 1-3
Trusting Heart

The Coming of Age Series
Running Its Course
Academia
The Coming of Age Series
Running Its Course

The Independent Women Series
Sleeping on Couches
Sequestered
Intermission
The Independent Women Series: Books 1-2

The Midwestern Series

The Heart of the Rodeo
The Flood Between Us
The Midwestern Series

The Survivor Series
Progress

Standalone
Starting Again
Food Truck Baby
Compassionate Minds
Beyond the Lights
◈◈◈◈◈◈◈◈◈◈◈◈◈◈◈◈
Gefühl für das Herz
Sentiment au Coeur
Sentimento al Cuore
Sentimento ao Coração
Sentimiento al Corazón
◈◈◈ ◈◈ ◈◈◈
◈◈◈◈◈
◈ ◈ ◈◈◈ ◈◈◈
Älä kerro kahdesti
İki Kere Söyleme
Moenie my twee keer vertel nie
Vertel het me niet twee keer
لا تقل لي مرتين
Не говори мне дважды
◈◈◈ ◈◈◈
Das Herz des Rodeo
Eine zweite Chance

Le Cœur du Rodéo
L'énigme de l'herbe à chat
Sag es mir nicht zweimal
Une brève débâcle
Un peu de cornichon
Bebê Caminhão de Comida
Camión de comida bebé
Food Truck Bambino
Food Truck Bébé
Imbisswagen Baby
Coeur de Confiance
Confiando en el Corazón
Coração de Confiança
Esprits
Mitfühlende Köpfe
Além da Luz
Au-Delà des Lumières
Más Allá de las Luces
Contenido del corazón
Contenu du cœur
Contenuto del cuore
Conteúdo do Coração
Herzenslust
Schlafen auf Sofas
Die Flut zwischen uns
El Diluvio Entre Nosotros
Il diluvio tra di noi
Le Déluge Entre Nous
O Dilúvio Entre Nós
From My Lips to Your Ears
The Mystery at Sherlock Lake
The Truth About Gravity
Cœur compliqué

Kompliziertes Herz
Ne Me le Dites Pas Deux Fois
Dormindo em Sofás
Dormir en sofás
Dormire sui divani
Dormir sur des canapés
Una Breve Debacle
Abgesondert
Secuestrado
Seqüestrado
Sequestrato
Séquestré
Une seconde chance
À batida de seu próprio tambor
Al ritmo de su propio tambor
Au rythme de leur propre tambour
Un Poco de un Pepinillo
Eine Stimme finden
El Enigma de Catnip
Encontrando uma voz
Encontrar una voz
Trovare una voce
Ein Fan, an den man sich erinnern sollte
Um fã para lembrar
Un fan à retenir
Un fan da ricordare
Un fan para recordar
Aspiración a afecto
Aspirante a afeto
Aspirante affetto
Strebende Zuneigung
Ein Sprungbrett
Un peldaño

Un trampolino di lancio
The Fashion Faux Pas
In Step
A Stalk Away
One Swipe Away
A Feline Matter: A Reagan Hummel Mystery
A Whisper of Truth
The Desk Job: A Monty Perez Mystery
The Oddball
Hallway Havoc
Because of You
Melting Into Your Arms
The Last Memory
The Heartbreaker

Watch for more at www.higginbothampublications.com.

About the Author

Growing up in a small town, Nicole Higginbotham-Hogue spent a majority of her time reading and writing, so when she was granted the opportunity to write full-time, she didn't have to think twice. Since beginning her writing career, she has managed to pen several lesbian romances, while adding a little action and adventure to spice things up. As a newly graduated MBA student, she plans to use her recently discovered free time to craft the art that she loves. For more information on Nicole's new releases or to find out what she has been working on, sign-up for her newsletter at higginbothampublications.com.

Read more at www.higginbothampublications.com.

Milton Keynes UK
Ingram Content Group UK Ltd.
UKHW011948160224
437951UK00001B/81